Chunky Girl

Book 1 in The Chunky Girl Chronicles

STORMY M. CORDERO

iUniverse, Inc.
New York   Bloomington

iUniverse books may be ordered through booksellers or by contacting:

iUniverse
1663 Liberty Drive
Bloomington, IN 47403
www.iuniverse.com
1-800-Authors (1-800-288-4677)

ISBN: 978-1-4401-6069-1 (sc)
ISBN: 978-1-4401-6070-7 (ebook)
ISBN: 978-1-4401-6071-4 (dj)

Printed in the United States of America

iUniverse rev. date: 8/20/2009

Table of Contents

1. Chunky

Being a teenage girl in America is pretty hard. Being shy, plump and clumsy just makes it that much more difficult. Combine those depressing facts with the most horrendous, spine chilling, humiliating nickname you could ever think of and... well... let's just say, life seems downright impossible! At least it does for me, Jenna Ella May or Chunky to everyone else.

Just hearing the name makes me cringe! The hateful nickname has followed me around for years. What once innocently began as a silly preschool game between my two best friends and me has now evolved into my worst nightmare. I curse the day my taste buds ever discovered chunky peanut butter! And I curse me when I remember how *I* came up with the bright idea of naming each of us Chunky; Peanut; Butter. So I don't even have the luxury of blaming anybody else but myself.

Now here I am 10 years later and the names have stuck. Fortunately though, for my best friends the names are a perfect fit. Tara, who is petite and tiny at five foot one, is the perfect Peanut. What she lacks in height, she makes up for in spunk. She is the most positive person I know and has been my best friend for my whole life! And her twin brother, Tommy, couldn't

1

ask for a better nickname than Butter. He's a husky footballer topping six feet and he can most definitely churn up a rival's offensive team with very little effort. Again, the name fits. Whereas Chunky... need I say more?

I have tried over the years to make the hated name go away, but no such luck. The name has stuck even worse than the chunky peanut butter we used to eat that stuck to the roof of our mouths! Not only has it stuck, it has also stained my life. During our elementary days, we easily referred to one another by our nicknames whether we were at home or school. Eventually our parents, classmates, and even our teachers began calling us by these names. That was all well and good 10 years ago, 8 years ago, and shoot, even 3 years ago, but now, on the eve of my junior year of high school and exactly 4 months after I turned 16... It royally sucks! And it sucks for a number of reasons.

First, I am a girl, and no girl I know of wants to be referred to as "chunky." Ever. Especially if said girl is, well, a little chunky. (Although I prefer the term "pleasantly plump." It just sounds cuter.) Second, well, being *chunky* would cover that one. And third, and I do believe most important, no guy is going to *ever* take a girl named Chunky seriously. It's like the name automatically relegates me to the category of "gal pal." That just sucks!

Other than Butter, who by the way does not count, I have never kissed a boy. It sounds kind of lame thinking about it, but the truth is it bothers me a lot. It's not like I want to be all slutty or anything remotely close to that, it's just that I want a little of what all the other girls seem to have. Attention and affection from someone that looks at them without thinking of bread and jelly. I want someone to find me interesting and appealing in a way that has nothing to do with me helping them get a better grade on a class project or study for a test. I want all the things a name like *Chunky* is not going to give me. And unless my dad gets transferred within the next 12 hours, it appears that my junior year will be a lot like every other year of my life!

Disgusted with myself and my somewhat self-deprecating thoughts, I threw myself down onto on my bed and reached over to my bedside table for my cell phone. Unfortunately, my hand hit my glass of water. I snatched at the glass but, of course, I was too late. The glass went flying and doused my new clock radio with its contents. In mere seconds the red numbers flickered and in less than ten seconds the whole thing completely shorted out.

"Great! Just great," I muttered to myself as I quickly got up to clean up the mess. This was my third alarm clock in less than a year. My dad was going to kill me and he was definitely going to quit letting me have anything to drink in my room. Not only that, I had to be up at six o'clock tomorrow morning and with no alarm clock, there was no way I was going to do that! Unless...

Picking up my cell phone, which had miraculously survived the shower, I hit speed dial for Peanut.

"Hey, girl! What's up?" I asked.

"I'm still picking out my outfit for tomorrow," she mumbled. I could hear shuffling, swishing and scraping in the background. It was obvious that she was trashing her closet. I cringed at the mess I couldn't see but that I knew most definitely existed. Peanut happens to be one of the messiest people I know.

"I thought you already decided on your new jeans and yellow t-shirt. As I recall, you said you were a junior now and you weren't going to make a big fuss about a new school year."

The sound of swooshing air assaulted my eardrum. "Chunky girl, don't start throwing my words back at me. I know what I said, but that was before I heard about these two new guys. They're brothers. One is a senior and the other is a junior. I am hearing some very exciting things about them!"

My interest definitely peaked I asked, "Like what? And where did you hear all these exciting things? If it's from Kristin...

3

well, you know you can't believe everything she tells you," I felt compelled to warn her before she got too far off on a tangent, as only Peanut is capable of.

Peanut's chuckle floated down the line and I had to smile in return. Peanut has an infectious laugh that makes me smile involuntarily, even if I don't happen to be very happy with her. It was something she knew about herself and often took advantage of.

"You don't have to remind me. I have not forgotten how much trouble she got me into when she told me about the lifeguard at our pool giving more than mouth-to-mouth resuscitation during CPR classes. She has never told a bigger lie, and stupid me, blurted it out right in the middle of a PTA meeting!"

I giggled, remembering that time all too well. I had tried to warn Peanut that I thought Kristin was making it all up. Unfortunately though, Peanut can be a bit tenacious when she believes something and as that particular lifeguard had played a bit fast and loose with her, she had been all too willing to believe the worst. Unfortunately again, that mistake had gotten her grounded for a whole month.

"Anyway," Peanut said, redirecting the conversation back to what she considered to be more important things. "Butter was at football practice this afternoon and these two guys showed up asking about trying out for the varsity football team. The older brother is a kicker and the younger brother is a quarterback."

I frowned, "But I thought Chad was our quarterback?" I didn't care too much for Chad. He had a way of saying "Chunky" that made it worse than it already was. He made it sleazy with a twist of insulting. He was the Wolverine quarterback, and I couldn't see him being very happy about sharing that roll. Chad was a jock with a capital J.O.C.K.

Peanut giggled a bit malevolently. She wasn't a big fan of Chad's either.

"He was," she said, "or I mean is. At least for now. But from what Butter was saying, Chad may have some real competition. It seems this new guy is really, really good."

"Hmm," I mused. Football at Mansfield High School was taken very seriously. The majority of the students attended the games religiously. Peanut and I never missed one, if for no other reason than to cheer on Butter who was a starter on defense. The Wolverines had missed the state championship last year by just one game. Butter had been crushed by the last minute loss, as had the entire school. There were high hopes that this year's team would get a second chance at the title. "This could get kind of ugly." I finally said.

"Yeah, I know. Butter said it was pretty obvious by the end of practice that Chad was ticked. He said Chad talked some smack with a few of the other guys on the team. He said that he could tell Chad was trying to stake his claim in front of the brothers."

That sounded like Chad, I thought to myself. He liked to win, he liked to be number one, and he liked wearing his black and gold number 7 Wolverine jersey. Unfortunately, those were the only things that seemed important to him. I'd often wondered why he was so popular and liked by all the cheerleaders. He didn't seem to have much to offer on a personal level.

"What did the brothers do?" I finally asked Peanut. "Did they say anything back? And what are their names, by the way? We can't keep saying 'the brothers' or 'the new guys.'"

"Their names are Dean and David. Butter said that they were pretty cool. David's the senior and Dean's the junior. Butter said that they just tried to pretend they couldn't hear what Chad was saying. He also said he overheard Dean tell David that they couldn't really blame Chad for being upset."

"Wow! That's pretty cool." I said to Peanut. Though frankly, I thought it was more than cool. Not many guys think things through or look at things with any kind of logical perspective. Teenage boys, in my opinion, were one step away from Cro-

Magnon man. When it came to their mentality, it was my experience that there wasn't much depth to what they thought or what they wanted.

"I thought so, too," Peanut chimed in bringing me back from my contemplation of the psyche of a teenage boy. "Now you know why I am having this whole wardrobe rethink. Looks like tomorrow may be about a little more than scholastics."

"Peanut, with your looks, you could wear Butter's clothes and still look hot."

Peanut laughed aloud at the mental image Chunky had created. "As big as he is, it wouldn't matter if I looked like Jessica Alba, I would look really stupid." I laughed along with her.

"Well, I'm not changing what I already picked out," I told her when we finally stopped laughing. "Besides, you told me it didn't make my butt look big. What more could I ask for?"

"Chunky, you need to shut up. The black tee you bought with those new jeans look great! Yeah, your butt may have a little more cushion, but I assure you, it was made to make jeans look good. Not the other way around."

"Okay. Okay," I cut in before Peanut started in on one of her 'Chunky you make me so mad sometimes' tirades. I refused to view myself in any other way but realistically and Peanut refused to acknowledge just what that way was. She was a great best friend even if she saw the world through rose colored glasses.

"You and Butter are still picking me up in the morning, right?"

"Of course we are."

"Good," I said. Then closing my eyes and taking a deep breath, I squeaked out, "I need one more tiny favor, though," I so dreaded having to ask for this particular favor. I hated having to divulge my clumsiness to anyone, even if that someone was Peanut.

"Sure. What do you need?"

"Could you call me when you get up? My umm... my alarm clock isn't working," I blurted out. I opened my eyes and stared at my toes as I waited for the predictable reaction.

"Chunky! What did you do this time? I swear that alarm clock couldn't be more than five months old!"

"Don't ask," I mumbled, refusing to give an explanation. I figured it should pretty much be self-explanatory as it was.

Peanut's giggles reverberated in my ear. Through that I could hear muffled speaking, before Peanut's giggles were replaced by Butter's deeper tones.

"Badaduntduntdunt, another one bites the dust?" Butter sang in his recently acquired baritone. I subconsciously noted that he phrased his question to the tune of the old Queen's song even as I listened to him continue to taunt me. "What did ya do this time, Chunky? Step on it, drop it, burn it?" he laughed down the line. He really was making *no* attempt to disguise his humor at my expense.

Even as embarrassed as I was, I couldn't help but start laughing along with him. As weird as it may seem, I am almost as close to Butter as I am Peanut. Their being twins superseded any mere sibling relationship. And somehow I am lucky enough to be enmeshed in that kinship, so that the three of us are intertwined into each other's lives.

"None of your business," I finally answered Butter when I stopped laughing.

"Well, if I had to guess, I'd say it was your classic glass of water by the bed. How many does that make this year? Ten?"

"Hey!" I yelled down the line at him. "Three. There have only been three! Stop exaggerating!"

Butter laughed some more. "Sorry," he sputtered. "My mistake. *Only* three. Just so you know though, Chunky, I've had the same alarm clock for the past five years."

"Now just a minute..." I started to yell down the line in mock anger but the muffled shuffling noises and Butter's muted guffaws told me he was no longer there.

Peanut's, "Save your breath," confirmed it.

"I swear, Peanut, if Butter runs his mouth tomorrow about those dumb alarm clocks I'm going to put pepper in his jock strap."

Peanut laughed. "As much as I would enjoy that I wouldn't recommend it. I did that once remember? And only once. Butter's forms of retribution can be extremely painful. Besides Chunky, everyone already knows that you can be somewhat... how do I put this delicately... somewhat inept at holding things... or picking up things... or walking places... or throwing things or..."

"Shut up Peanut! I get your point. It's just a new year you know. I want it to be different. *I* want to be different."

"Why Chunky? I like you just the way you are," Peanut said with deep sincerity. "There isn't another you in this entire world. You need to appreciate that about yourself."

I smiled to myself. I loved Peanut. With Peanut I *could* really appreciate being Chunky. "You know what I mean, Peanut."

"Yeah, I know," she quietly agreed. "I know. We'll pick you up in the morning."

"Don't forget the wakeup call!" I interrupted, before she could say goodbye.

Peanut scoffed, "As if I could!" before hanging up the phone.

I held the silent cell phone to my ear for long moments before I flipped it shut. For a minute I contemplated going back through my wardrobe and possibly finding something a little more...well *more*. For a split second I tried to imagine the new brothers. It was pretty obvious Peanut was psyched about something, which meant they were probably not only gifted with great football skills, but that they were gorgeous and smart, too. Which of course, meant they weren't likely to be enthralled by one Jenna Ella May, Chunky girl extraordinaire.

Nah, I thought, I would not spend any more time picking out what I was going to wear. The outfit I'd already picked was about as good as it was going to get. What I needed to do was spend a little more time on my prayers tonight—praying that my inescapable companion "clumsiness" would miraculously disappear, to be replaced by "grace" and "poise." It also wouldn't hurt to ask that those new jeans I planned on wearing tomorrow be a little looser than normal when I put them on. And, if at all possible, that I'd experience an inexplicable growth spurt of approximately two inches. Yeah, I had some serious praying to do tonight. Like I said, being a teenage girl growing up in America today bites!

2. First Day of School

The musical lyrics of Snow Patrol's "Chasing Cars" invaded my surprisingly pleasant first day. There had been no mishaps or major crises to mar what was a pretty great first day so far. And it appeared the day was about to get better because there was Butter walking my way with two guys I didn't recognize, which could only mean one thing. Butter was about to bring the two new brothers over to me and introduce us. How cool is Butter? I knew I liked him for a reason.

I started to place a big smile on my face, but just as quickly it was replaced by confusion, then dismay. I wasn't about to meet anybody, I realized. The music wasn't coming from the kid with the IPod standing next to me in the hallway, but my cell phone. It was the ringer for Peanut. She was giving me my wake up call.

Stuffing my head deep into my pillow I growled my disappointment. I should have known that the first day wouldn't go that smoothly for me. Without lifting my head, I reached out and grabbed the offending item, which continued to play "Chasing Cars", and stuck it to my ear.

"I'm up."

"Wow! Don't you sound excited!" Peanut's too cheerful voice shrilled at me.

"Bad dream," I replied, before quickly changing it. "I mean good dream."

"Well, which one was it?"

"Good. It was definitely good. Unfortunately it was a dream. I just hope it's not some kind of ironic message from the Powers That Be."

"Okay Chunky, you lost me after unfortunately... but you don't have to explain," she quickly assured me. "Get your butt up out of bed and get dressed. Butter wants to leave a little earlier. He said he's meeting someone at school."

"Who?" I quizzed quickly flashing to my dream.

"Eric," Peanut answered, dashing any hopes that there was even the tiniest possibility that some of my dream could come true. I'm not a psychic after all, and it *was* just a dream. But a girl could still always hope.

Silently groaning, I ended my call with Peanut and jumped out of bed heading directly for my bathroom. I absolutely had to wash my hair every morning before I left the house otherwise it stuck flat to my head and looked greasy. Without much fuss I was in and out of the shower before I ever heard my dad moving around.

My dad is a great guy. Whereas, most girls my age get embarrassed by their dads, I don't. Probably because my dad is not only my dad: but my dad *and* my mom. My mom left us when I was two. And when I say left us, I mean she packed her bags and left Greenville, North Carolina without seemingly taking one glance back. As a result, I really don't remember her and most days I really don't even want to. I have my dad and there is none better. Why wish for something you never really had and didn't miss?

Walking back into my bedroom I grabbed up the jeans I planned to wear. Closing my eyes with a silent last appeal, I began putting them on. In seconds I knew that at least one prayer wasn't going to be answered. There was no way these jeans were looser than before. If anything, they felt a little snugger. Not a good sign.

Dismissing any negative thoughts with determination, I slipped on my tee, smoothing it down over my stomach and hips. Stepping back a few steps, I gave myself the once over in the full length mirror behind my bedroom door.

Not bad. But not great either. I'm short. I'm plump. I have full breasts and even fuller hips. This kind of figure at the age of sixteen can be difficult to live with. My generous and very notable curves make me feel a little more than self-conscious.

I smoothed my hand down over my tummy. I did have a great waist, though. No love handles for me. Unfortunately the downside of this was that the smallness of my waist highly accentuated the roundness of what came above and below. This is why I never wear short shirts of any kind.

With a last critical glance I walked back into the bathroom to blow-dry my straight, shoulder-length brown hair into its habitual style. Adding a bit of mascara, lip gloss, and mineral powder I was ready to go. Thankfully, not one zit had made a late-night appearance. Although miraculously blessed with a pretty decent complexion, it wouldn't have shocked me if I had woken up with a full—all-out breakout.

Snatching up my surprisingly full book bag, I headed towards the kitchen where I could hear my dad banging around. For some reason that escapes me, he continues to insist on making me a full breakfast on the first day of school. Considering I very rarely eat breakfast, I find it even more confusing, but I make an effort of eating at least half of it. I can't bring myself to hurt his feelings, which is funny, because if you look at my dad you would probably think no one could hurt him.

My dad, Royal May, stands about six feet three inches in his stocking feet and weighs about a ton, a ton of solid muscle and no fat. He used to play college football for Appalachian State University before a knee injury knocked him out of the game for good. So he finished his college education and majored in criminology. He is a police detective now. *I* sure wouldn't mess with him.

"Morning Chunky," my dad said leaning over and placing a quick kiss on my cheek.

I had been about to reciprocate my morning salutations until I heard the hated nickname. I winced instead. "I wish everyone would stop calling me that. I'm not a kid anymore."

I could tell my dad was hiding a smile because he quickly turned his back toward me before speaking. "Well, as far as you not being a kid anymore... well... we'll just agree to disagree. As for the name thing... if you don't want people to call you that, just tell them so."

I rolled my eyes. I hadn't realized my dad was so naive. "Yeah Dad, you're right. Why hadn't I thought of that? I'll tell everyone not to do it and they will all magically stop because hey, they're sweet, nice biddable high school kids after all. They don't ever tease or harass or make fun of anyone. It might hurt someone's feelings you know. "

"Sarcasm noted and not appreciated Chunky."

I grinned at him unrepentantly. "Sorry."

"Yeah, I can tell," he said grinning back at me. "Eat your breakfast."

Silence reigned in the kitchen for the next few minutes while I tried to swallow down scrambled eggs and toast. My dad apparently wasn't having any trouble in that department. He finished his off before attacking my plate after asking me if I was finished. Glad to not have to pretend I was interested in eating the food remaining on my plate, I handed it over.

"Are Butter and Peanut picking you up in that thing he likes to call a car?"

I smiled. Dad and Butter had a longstanding disagreement about the Honda Civic hatchback that Butter drove. It really wasn't any particular color. I think it might have been red at one time but now it was mainly rust. Butter's grandfather and he had worked on it since Butter was fourteen and Butter loved that car. He even named it Princess. He said she had personality and a regal bearing (whatever that meant). Peanut and I just humored him.

"Yes. They should be here any minute. Peanut called me this morning and told me they would be here a little earlier than usual because Butter is meeting someone this morning."

My dad gave me his cryptic detective look, eyebrow cocked, lips pursed and baldhead shining. "Did she only call to tell you that or could there be another reason she *needed* to call you?"

I looked back at him in all innocence. "I haven't a clue as to what you could be referring to," I answered in a fake British, upper crust-like accent. I stood with my shoulders pulled rigidly back, eyebrows raised and a very haughty expression on my face.

Dad cocked his eyebrow at me and crossed his arms over his chest. "Very cute," he sarcastically complimented me on my dramatic performance, before lowering both brows to squint at me in a look he had perfected over the years while dealing with criminals. It was a look that warned whoever was on the opposing end of it: 'don't give me any of your crap.'

We stared at each other across the kitchen floor in silence for long moments, before Dad uncrossed his arms and lazily leaned back against the kitchen counter. I knew better than to let down my guard despite his lazy stance. Dad's tactics could be sneaky.

"I didn't hear your alarm clock go off this morning," he remarked oh so casually and quite innocently. I knew I had been smart to remain leery of him.

"Maybe you slept through it," I answered just as casually, as I slowly backed out of the kitchen. "You know," I continued in the same mock casualness. "You are getting older and I hear your hearing is one of the first things to go. You might want to get your ears checked." I made a quick, almost desperate grab for my book bag and headed straight out the kitchen door. "See you when you get home!" I called to him over my shoulder.

Just as I was about to close the door behind me I heard, "Chunky!"

I stopped immediately but I didn't turn around. I knew what was coming after all. "Yes sir?"

"I'll pick you up a new alarm clock on my way home tonight."

I sighed aloud, my shoulders drooped just the slightest bit in hopelessness. What was the point in trying to deny my reality? "Thanks Dad," I said, glancing back and over at him. "I think maybe we should invest some stock in alarm clocks. At the rate I'm going, you could be a millionaire by the time I graduate college."

Dad chuckled at my lame joke. "Have a good day, honey."

"Thanks Dad. I'll try. And you be careful," I tacked on as was my ritual. I secretly feared that if I ever once forgot to tell him to be careful when he left for work that that would be the day something awful would happen to him.

"Always," he answered back as was his ritual and hearing that *one* word comforted me more than anything else he could have said. I think that the word "always" is my most favorite word of all.

Just as I closed the kitchen door behind me, I heard Butter's car pull into my driveway. Peanut waved at me from the front passenger seat, while Butter made motioning movements with his hands that pretty much indicated he didn't think I was moving fast enough.

I poked my tongue out at him as I walked past his window before opening the back door and climbing in. "Patience is a virtue, Butter," I gently scolded him in my best schoolmarm's voice.

"You know what you can do with your patience, Chunky," Butter muttered back, before backing out of my driveway at a speed I hoped my dad hadn't noticed.

"Jeez Butter," Peanut groaned, apparently having the same

15

thought as me. "I hope Detective Royal didn't see that. You know he'll be on the phone to Dad in a second."

Butter immediately slowed the car to a more respectable pace. "Sorry," he groaned as he looked into his rearview mirror as if my dad chasing him down was a real possibility. "I'm in a hurry to see Eric."

"You want to see Eric about what?"

"He has some tickets to the Cold Play concert that he's trying to sell. Evidently his dad's company is having some kind of big deal banquet the same night and his dad is making him attend."

Peanut squealed with excitement as soon as she heard the name of the group. "How many tickets does he have?" she asked then quickly added, "You are including Chunky and me in on this aren't you?"

Butter rolled his eyes at me in the rearview mirror. I couldn't help but grin back at him. He wasn't fooling me in the least. He may be a boy and Peanut may be a girl but that didn't come between these two. They were twins and they were solid. I thank my lucky stars every day that by some stroke of luck they were willing to include me in on that bond.

"Butter?" Peanut growled, punching him lightly in the arm. "There will be tickets enough for Chunky and me right?"

"Hey!" Butter exclaimed rubbing his arm as if the punch hurt. "That hurt," he pouted at her. She just rolled her eyes back at him. "Well?"

"Of course it does idiot. Do you think I don't know that I wouldn't get any peace for the next two months if I got tickets to see Cold Play and didn't take you two with me to see them? I just as soon lay on top of a mound of fire ants," he exclaimed dramatically. "Naked!" he emphasized in exaggerated horror, "than go without you two."

Peanut and I giggled as Butter continued his one man monologue the rest of the way to school.

My stomach started to form little butterflies as soon as

we reached school. I noticed, as Butter turned into the school parking lot, that the large boulder that sat at the entrance of our school was freshly painted black with gold letters spelling out Wolverines.

As was typical for the first day of school, the parking lots were packed with cars going in every direction; students, parents, and teachers buzzed around disoriented: Quite simply chaos reigned. The butterflies got larger.

"Where in the world am I going to park?" Butter muttered to himself as he drove down yet another aisle.

"I'm really glad it's not supposed to rain today," Peanut murmured, glancing out her window and up towards the sky. "If you end up having to park all the way back here, we'd get soaked."

I glanced up out of the window at the blue, blue sky. There wasn't a cloud in sight. The only color, other than blue, was the large ball of yellow-orange fire that glowed so brightly I wished I'd remembered to bring my sunglasses.

"Got one!" Butter suddenly exclaimed in triumph as he whipped into a vacant space. Peanut and I applauded and cheered his efforts.

In mere seconds we were all out of the car and walking toward the quad. Though the three of us were the best of friends, we all had other friends and people we'd known for years. The quad is the spot we usually met up with them to talk and catch up.

The quad was by the junior, senior parking lot so we didn't have far to walk, as opposed to last year when we were sophomores. The sophomore parking lot is on the other side of the school and we used to have to leave home about ten minutes earlier than we did today just to get there. Being a junior definitely came with some perks, I decided.

As we got closer to where a group of our friends stood, my stomach started doing that churning thing it sometimes does. For some reason I always dreaded this moment. Though I'd known most of these people for most of my life, I always felt self-conscious and under the microscope. Summer is almost three months and a lot can happen in that time, not to mention change (especially bra cup sizes.) So it's here that the guys start taking mental notes of all those changes. Some did it discreetly while others not so much. I really wasn't comfortable with anyone taking notice of the changes that had taken place with me one way or the other, and most especially not this year as I'd grown two cup sizes over the summer. I'd have preferred to keep it a secret but boobs have a funny way of popping out, standing up, and sometimes almost even waving, hi. I crossed my hands over my chest as we approached a group.

Everyone started talking at once and hi's and how are you's were passed around from person to person. In moments I began to relax and let my guard down. This wasn't going to be that bad after all, I decided while laughing at something Eric was saying to Butter. No one was looking at me as if I was gross or disgusting or too fat to live. Everyone appeared to find nothing wrong in my jeans that were a bit too snug. Everything was going to be okay.

"Chunky!" a high pitched voice squealed from several feet away. "Chunky!" it rang out again as if in accusation rather than attention seeking. The voice was so loud that everyone stopped talking. All eyes swung to the older lady calling out to me before, in tandem, they all swept back to me with eyebrows raised and their eyes taking me in. In that moment I knew every single junior and senior at Mansfield High School knew exactly *how* snug my jeans were today.

The first day of school was going to suck.

3. Have a Nice Trip

For about five seconds I stood as if made from stone, a red stone. My face was absolutely flaming in embarrassment. I could hear whispers and a few muffled chuckles. I felt eyes galore staring at me, boring into me. Now I'm not going to say that some of those eyes weren't kind because they were. Peanut and Butter looked shocked and upset for me. They knew how much I abhorred being the center of attention, and Mrs. Drysdale had more than placed me at the center of attention this morning.

"Chunky dear," Mrs. Drysdale called out yet again, while bustling her way over to me. Now you'd have to see Mrs. Drysdale to really appreciate her. She is about five feet one and weighs about one hundred pounds soaking wet. She's also about seventy years old with white as snow hair that sticks out all over the place. She is the school's librarian. No one ever got away from Mrs. Drysdale when she called for them, and it appeared that today was no exception.

"Why Chunky, haven't you grown this summer?" Mrs. Drysdale continued in her overly loud manner. I knew she wasn't saying I'd grown chunky over the summer but the *way* she said it made everyone give me a good glance over, the very thing I'd wanted to avoid. I refused to make eye contact with anyone at that moment. I finally understood what it meant to want the earth to open up and swallow you whole. If only I could be so lucky.

"I'm going to need help with some art work in the library and Mr. Singleton said you'd be the person I would want to talk to. That young man said you have quite a talent."

Cheeks still boasting a hateful reddish sheen, I quickly glanced up and agreed to help her. For God's sake, I would have agreed to almost anything at that moment if it would have gotten her to leave.

"You're such a good girl, Chunky," Mrs. Drysdale praised me, patting me on the back of my hand with her tiny fingers, before fluttering off to wreak havoc in someone else's unsuspecting life.

An awkward kind of silence existed for a few moments after Mrs. Drysdale's departure, before some kind soul took pity on me and began talking. I could still hear a few muted giggles but I'm honest enough to admit that it could have been my own paranoia, assuming that the giggles were at my expense.

"Oh, Chunky," Peanut whispered as she made her way back over to me. Peanut knew better than anyone how I hated being made the center of attention. "Are you okay?"

I rolled my eyes at her in response. Now that the worst was over, I could finally feel that hateful blush receding from my cheeks. "Guess it could have been worse," I said. I really wanted to pretend that I wasn't that bothered. I really wanted to *be* not that bothered. When would I ever outgrow these stupid hang-ups I had? When could I be like all the other girls around me? They were never bothered by things like this. "She could have gotten my nickname confused and called me fatty."

Peanut glared back at me. "That's not funny Chunky. You are not fat!"

"Did Butter get the tickets?" I quickly asked Peanut. I wanted desperately to change the subject. The last thing I needed was for anyone to overhear a conversation like that. If they did, I felt quite sure that a couple of Dr. Phil cracks would be headed my way. No thank you.

Luckily it appeared I had asked the right question. Peanut launched into a funny version of how Butter had begged and pleaded to have first dibs at the tickets. While she was telling the story I could feel the hairs on the back of my neck stand straight up. It wasn't exactly the most comfortable of feelings. It was actually a little creepy.

I started to glance around as discreetly as I could. I wanted to know who was staring at me but I didn't want *them* to know I wanted to know. After glancing first left then right, I tried a half- turn while swinging my arm around as if to massage my shoulder. It was then I saw Chad. I saw Chad and he was watching me. As quickly as possible I turned back around to Peanut who was almost finished with her story.

I let her wind down before whispering, "Is Chad still staring at me?"

Peanut looked at me in shock at first, but Peanut is no dummy. Within a second she had sized up everything. "Yeah he is."

"Is it still in that creepy way?" I asked. I couldn't exactly describe how he looked, other than creepy. He looked drawn to me, but extremely ticked off about it at the same time.

"Unfortunately, yeah, he is. I wonder what his problem is. He better not mess with you."

I laughed aloud at hearing Peanut voice her last thought. Her protectiveness helped to soothe away the heinous last moments of my life and Chad's odd behavior. The bell suddenly rang and we started making our way to our classes. In the shuffle and bustle I didn't have time to give Chad or Mrs. Drysdale another thought.

As it was, I only had time to concentrate on making it across campus in record time. Mr. Smith's biology classroom had been moved over the summer and the last thing I wanted was to be late on the first day. Regardless what a lot of kids my age thought, my dad was more than right when he said first impressions counted. And being late wasn't going to be very impressive.

Walking as fast as I could without actually running, I made it to class with seconds to spare. Flying in through the classroom door I bolted for the empty desk I saw towards the back of the room. My eyes were so focused on the desk that I didn't see the handles of the book bag sprawled out in the aisle. Not, that is, until my Sketchers got caught in one and I went sprawling belly down, butt up onto the floor. Great, I thought to myself, so much for first impressions.

Deafening silence proceeded my bumbling fall to be replaced immediately by muted laughter and snickers. I decided at that moment, that my dream last night was definitely chock full of irony.

As I started to get up, I heard a chair scrape back. In the next moment I felt large hands grab me up under my elbows and haul me up off my feet, before placing me gently back down. Those same large, and now I'm noticing *warm,* hands then slid from my elbows up to my shoulders to steady me on my feet.

"I am so sorry," a voice said from at least a foot above my own head. "Are you okay?"

As mortified as I was about not only falling down face first but by being literally picked up off my feet, I couldn't resist the temptation of looking up into the face of the boy who had the voice of an angel. I mentally gave myself a shake at my silly poetic thoughts, silently wondering if maybe I'd conked myself on the head, when I suddenly made eye to eye contact with the prettiest blue eyes I had ever seen. They were crystal blue and surrounded by the thickest lashes. They were also the eyes of a stranger. A knot formed in the pit of my stomach. I was pretty sure I knew who this was going to turn out to be. What was it I said earlier about first impressions?

"Are you okay?" I was asked again. Unfortunately, this time

the question was accompanied with a very light shake, followed by a look that said, "She either hit her head pretty hard or else she's not all here."

"Oh yeah... umm... I'm fine," I finally gathered my wits enough to answer, before taking a step back away from the strong hands. "Umm..." I had no idea what I was about to say.

I stood there dumbly, glancing around at everything and everyone which was probably why Mr. Smith felt compelled to ask, "Chunky, are you okay? Do you need to see the school nurse?"

Unfortunately, I was looking directly at the new guy when Mr. Smith started talking. And *unfortunately*, I saw the new guy frown when Mr. Smith called me Chunky, to be quickly proceeded by a very thorough once over of my person, which brought on another case of the blushes. But most unfortunately, I stood there in shock when said new guy jumped to my defense after misunderstanding why Mr. Smith called me Chunky.

"Excuse me sir, no offense, but I think it's rude for you to call her that."

Shocked silence descended over the entire room before almost hysterical laughter followed close behind. Poor Mr. Smith, the new guy, and I were the only ones not enjoying this predicament. I could tell Mr. Smith wanted to explain himself but wasn't quite sure how to go about it without disturbing the class—or me—further.

I, myself, would just have preferred to let the entire matter go with no explanation, but that would only have lead to more embarrassment later on down the road. As it was, the guy had tried to defend me. He seemed to be a decent boy. He may secretly agree that I'm chunky, but it didn't mean he was going to let a person abuse me with it. That in it-self earned him a brief and quiet explanation.

"It's my nickname. There's a long story about how I came by it, but it's what everyone calls me. Mr. Smith wasn't being mean. It's not his fault that it happens to be true." And with that, and without another glance into those gorgeous eyes, I picked my book bag up off the floor and with as much poise as I could muster; I sat down in the empty desk behind him. Thankfully, Mr. Smith decided to grasp control back from the unruly juniors and began a long drawn out explanation of biology and all that it entailed.

While he droned on, I slouched down into my chair and stared at the back of the new guy's head. Dean. I was pretty sure that that was what Peanut had said his name was. David was the senior, so he would be taking physics this year.

Barely seeing past my humiliation, I couldn't help but notice that Dean had great hair. It was a dark rich brown, cropped close to his head but a little longer and spikier on top. Of course, I knew his hair would keep me occupied for only so long before the whole disastrous encounter began to replay over and over again in my mind. I really, really, *really* couldn't believe that I had actually tacked on the last part of what I'd said to him. How in the world could I have said it wasn't Mr. Smith's fault if it was true? Why would I do that? Wasn't it bad enough that Dean had already made it clear that he thought I was chunky, without me telling him it's okay to acknowledge it? I don't care how true it is. Acknowledging being fat with one of the hottest guys I have ever seen is plain stupid. I really couldn't see how I would ever be able to face him again. Not that I would have too, at least not that much. With his looks and his apparent talent on the field, he really wouldn't be hanging out with me anyway, especially after today.

The class seemed endless. Every five minutes felt like fifteen. Dean seemed to be pretty fidgety. I noticed him glance back at me a couple of times, but I made sure I was looking off in another direction before his crystal eyes came into contact with my brown ones. As much as I would have liked a few extra minutes to appreciate the beauty that was Dean, there was just no way in Hades that I was going to risk it with the way my luck has been going.

Thirty seconds before the bell was to ring, I slipped my book bag over my shoulder in preparation for a speedy exit. I had the feeling new guy wanted to apologize and I really didn't want to give him a chance. The sooner he forgot what happened the better off I'd be, though I knew it would be a long time, if ever, before my mind allowed me the same luxury.

Five, four, three, two one, I counted off. As soon as the bell rang I zipped out ahead of everyone and headed straight for Spanish class. Thankfully, Peanut would be in this class with me. I *so* needed her tiny petite shoulders to lean on.

Of course, as luck would have it, Peanut didn't arrive until almost before the bell. I could tell by the expression on her face that she had already heard about my first period exploits.

"Did it hurt?" she asked, confirming my suspicions.

"My body or my ego?" I asked back, leaving her in no doubt which one I considered to be more bruised.

"Either? Both?" she guessed.

"You pick," I suggested. "How much did you hear?"

"You fell. Mr. Smith called you Chunky. New guy thought Mr. Smith was being insulting and so new guy defended you," she answered, ticking each item of interest off on a finger.

"Yeah," I confirmed, nodding my head. "But did you hear the part where I explained to new guy why Mr. Smith referred to me as Chunky and how it wasn't Mr. Smith's fault that I really happened to be chunky?"

Peanut groaned aloud, closing her eyes and slapping her palm across them in dismay. "Oh, Chunky, you really are your own worst enemy. Why did you have to go and say something like that?"

Though I felt like crying, I refused to give into the lame luxury. "Because," I said more forcefully than I intended. "It was pretty obvious that he considered me fat and I wanted him to know I already knew I was. I wanted him to know that I wasn't deluding myself into thinking anything else. I wanted him to know that--- I. Already. Knew."

25

"Chunky, you tick me off sometimes, you know that? You really do," Peanut said and it was obvious she was getting herself really worked up. "You. Are. Not. Fat!" she growled back at me pretty much the same way I had at her. "You are plump, hippy, voluptuous, phat but you are not fat! Now I'm sorry, but I'm your best friend and I'm going to tell you like it is. I'm sorry. I'm *really* sorry that you tripped in class. I know that that must have been really embarrassing. And I can even see how the misunderstanding might have been a bit embarrassing for you as well, but the rest of it—the part you seem more upset about than any other part... that's of your own making... of your own self-consciousness. And that's on you. You told me yesterday you wanted this year to be different. You said that *you* want to be different. Well, be different!"

I wasn't given a chance to respond because the bell rang at that moment. I wasn't even sure what I would have said anyway. Peanut was right after all. I was more upset about the things that had actually been in my control rather than the things that had not. I did need to make some self-image changes, but for the life of me, I really didn't know how or where to begin.

4. Dean

Thankfully, my next two classes were quite uneventful. Even more promising was the fact that Dean wasn't in either of those classes so I hadn't had to face him. Though I knew I would eventually have to, it was nice knowing I was being given a little time to regroup. At least one thing was going my way today.

Fourth period bell rang releasing the junior class for lunch. Peanut and I had agreed earlier to meet each other outside the cafeteria before looking for a place to sit. She and I both brown bagged it. We refused to eat the tasteless mess that was served in school. As I approached the cafeteria I could see Peanut was already there, and she wasn't alone. She was surrounded by a group consisting of Butter, Eric, Nathan, Tina, Jamie and... Dean.

I gulped audibly. I could handle this. This was no big deal. Yes, it was embarrassing, I acknowledged to myself, but move on. Besides, I assured myself, I'm sure he already had.

"Hey, hey, hey Chunky!" Butter said, grabbing me by the hand and dragging me inside with him. "I thought you'd never get here. I'm starved!" he continued to grouse, before quickly tucking me in under his arm and murmuring, "Sorry. I heard about earlier this morning. Dean really seems like a nice guy.

27

You have to admit it was pretty cool of him defending you and all. Anyway... sit by me and I'll keep you distracted."

"Thanks Butter," I whispered, giving him a quick squeeze before heading to an empty table, while he got in line for food. Butter loved school pizza. He said he could eat it every day, for breakfast, lunch, and dinner if only someone would let him. I shuddered at even the thought of having to eat it once a year.

As I sat down and started pulling food out of my lunch bag, I thought about what Butter had said. I mean *really* thought about it. I had been so caught up in my misery of this morning I'd never taken the time to appreciate what Dean had done for me this morning. Defending someone was always cool. But to defend someone you didn't know while being a new kid at a new school in front of a bunch of strange peers and to a teacher no *less* was really pretty amazing. And here I was trying to avoid him as if he had done something wrong, when he deserved no less than a thank you, from me.

I was so caught up in my introspection that it took me a second to realize that everyone else had already sat down around me, and were busy eating and talking to each other. It took me only half a second later to realize that it wasn't Peanut on the other side of me, but Dean and he appeared to be waiting for me to notice him sitting there.

"I'm Dean," he introduced himself. "Dean Scott."

"I'm..." I started awkwardly, before cutting off abruptly. How was I supposed to tell *him* to call me Chunky?

My eyes shot around the table, searching for Peanut, who I had just assumed would be sitting beside me, before looking back at Dean.

Dean gave a huff of laughter. Not mean, but as if he understood and commiserated. "Yeah, I know. You're um... Ch... Chunky," he finished for me in somewhat of an awkward stammer and his eyes, for a moment, darted away from mine. It was almost as if he didn't like or was uncomfortable with calling me Chunky, I thought to myself. Then he held up his hand toward me, palm out. "Don't worry," he assured me in firmer tone. "I'm not going to ask how you came by that name. Butter already gave me a full explanation and I must admit it was a pretty creative one. Unusual," he added with a grin. "But very, very unique."

I smiled back at him while my fingers played nervously with my bottle of water. It was obvious he was trying to gloss over this morning's debacle and I truly appreciated his consideration. "Probably not one of my better ideas though," I answered back.

Dean grinned down at me. He had a very boyish grin with beautiful pearly white teeth and dimples in each cheek. Dean was almost pretty. I had to keep reminding myself not to stare. Taking a glance around the lunchroom it was pretty obvious that I wasn't the only girl afflicted with the same problem.

"Thank you, by the way," I started to say, before I had to stop and clear my throat. For some reason it felt very constricted and dry. I took a quick swig from my bottle of water and started again. "Thanks for standing up for me. You didn't know me and you didn't have to do it, so thank you."

"You're very welcome," he responded graciously. "But I did, you know," he said, glancing down at me before biting into his sandwich.

"You did what?" I asked, while watching him. He even looked adorable chewing. Most guys looked like Butter when they ate, gobbling down food with no decorum, but for some reason Dean didn't.

"I had to defend you," he stated quite simply. "If he really had been saying what I thought, then that would have been unacceptable, and I would have had to defend you."

"Why?" I asked with curiosity.

A frown instantly appeared on his face. "Why not?"

"Good point," I finally answered after a moment of contemplation. He was obviously trying to tell me he did it because it was the right thing to do. I couldn't argue with what he was saying so I didn't even try.

In the next moment Eric and Butter pulled Dean into a conversation about football. As much as I wanted to keep talking with Dean, I was glad of the respite. Having Dean's full attention was a bit intense. When Dean talked with you, *he talked with you*. He gave you his full attention. I knew myself well enough to know that I could crush on this guy in a big way and as the chances of him reciprocating that affection were pretty slim, I would only wind up hurting myself.

As Dean talked with the guys I finally made eye contact with Peanut who sat on the other side of Butter. She motioned for me to lean back in my seat. When I did I was greeted by an impish smile and wink.

"I thought we were going to sit together?" I whispered across Butter's back while ignoring her smug look.

"I thought you'd rather sit with him," Peanut responded with the slightest nod of her head in Dean's direction. I blushed. I couldn't deny it.

Eric claimed Peanut's attention then, and I went back to eating my lunch. It was while I was chewing my Subway turkey sub that I got that same strange prickly sensation on the back of my neck. Someone was staring at me and I wondered if it was Chad again. As unobtrusively as I could, I started glancing around the cafeteria. I didn't have to glance far, before making direct eye to eye contact with Chad. He held my eyes for a few seconds before glancing at Dean, then back at me. His lips smirked and it was obvious that Chad was thinking smutty thoughts. It became more than obvious when his eyes traveled back to me before lowering to my chest, where they paused indecently and for far too long, before coming back up to meet mine. The smirk had turned into a sneer and I felt my face turn hot in mortification.

I sucked in a deep gulp of air. It was only then that I became aware of the fact that I had stopped breathing during the entire exchange. Dean turned his head quickly to look down at me. "Are you all right?" he asked, noticing my high color and labored breathing.

I couldn't bring myself to look up at him. I didn't want him to see the shame or confusion I was feeling. I didn't have the slightest clue what was going on with Chad this year. He had never been one of my favorite guys, but he'd never been like this before... so nasty and downright insulting without even saying a word.

"Hello?" Dean said, waving his hand in front of my face. I got the idea that this was not the first time he'd tried to get my attention.

"Yo Chunky?" Butter called from across the table. "What's up?" he asked, as he leaned over toward me.

It was then that I noticed that everyone at our table was staring at me now. No one was talking. They all appeared to be waiting for some sort of response, or at the very least, an explanation from me.

I forced a laugh past my tense lips and made eye contact with first Butter then Dean. "Sorry, I was a million miles away."

"No kidding," Butter mumbled, sitting back in his chair with a flop. "It took us for ever to get your attention. What were you thinking about?"

"I was making a mental list for all the extra school supplies I need to pick up," I hedged.

Fortunately for me, it appeared everyone accepted my lame explanation. Everyone except for Peanut, that was. She was giving me one of her looks. The one that told me I would have some explaining to do later.

Grumbles rumbled around the table. Glancing at my watch, I realized what all the grumbles were about. Lunch was about to end and fifth period to begin. I started gathering my trash together to carry to the trash bin.

As I started to get up from my seat, a long arm reached

over my shoulder. "Here, I got that," Dean said swiping my trash and walking away before I could say a word. I was a bit surprised at first, but quickly realized he was just being nice. He was probably trying to make up for earlier, though he really hadn't done anything wrong.

I peeked around to see if anyone else noticed or found it strange. Thankfully, everyone else was busy doing their own thing and they weren't paying attention to me. Everyone but Peanut, that was. She was waggling her eyebrows up and down at me, and grinning like the Cheshire cat. I rolled my own eyes back at her. I wasn't about to get caught up in any imaginary Peanut drama. No way. No how. Huh-uh! I was about to go over there and tell her exactly that when Dean unexpectedly appeared back at my side.

"Um...Thanks," I said a tad bit awkwardly. He was staring down at me expectantly and for the life of me I couldn't figure out what he wanted or what he was waiting for. "For taking my trash," I clarified when he continued to stand there.

Pearly teeth flashed and dimples appeared. God he had a great smile.

"I know. And you're welcome," he added while staring down at me from a height I was guessing was about six feet two. As I'm not quite five feet three, I had to look pretty far up. Somehow though, I really didn't mind it in the least.

"What's your next class?" he finally prompted when it became apparent I wasn't going to say anything else.

"Oh... um... U.S. History with Ms. Miller," I said while mentally berating myself to get it together. I talked to guys all the time. One of my very best friends is a teenage guy. What in the world was my problem that I couldn't carry on a simple conversation with this one?

Dean's dimples grew more pronounced. "Yeah? That's great, so do I. Here you go," he added and before I knew it, he was picking up my book bag and helping to hook it over my shoulder. "I guess we better start heading in that direction if we don't want to be late."

I caught Peanut's eye as Dean and I started walking away from the table. She gave me a little sign with her hands telling me to go on with him before doing a little, call me later impression with her fingers. I gave her a quick nod to let her know I would. Just as Dean and I made it about four steps, the intercom speakers popped into life and a nasally voice was requesting the presence of one Dean Scott to please make an appearance in the office.

Dean stopped mid-stride and glanced down at me. "That's me. I better go see what they need."

"Sure," I said, nodding my head up and down at him in understanding. "I'll... um... I'll see you around," I said offhandedly, hoping and praying like crazy that he couldn't see the disappointment I was feeling. I mean, I know we were just walking to class together. It wasn't like he'd asked me out on a date or something. But it was nice having the cute new guy obviously wanting to get to know me. The fact was it was pretty darn exhilarating.

Dean cocked his head at me quizzically before shaking it quickly and flashing his (what I was starting to think of as) infamous grin, saying only, "I'll see you around," before walking off toward the office.

Deflated was what I felt as I started my lonely trek to U.S. History---which was silly, really. I had no business getting so worked up about something so little. Every time I was around Dean it became more apparent that he was simply a really nice guy. He had manners and a moral code and a killer smile. It was easy to see why I was reacting like this to him. Most likely, all the girls in school were feeling the same way, too. I needed to rein myself in and not take these small little gestures of friendship as anything more personal. That road led to heartache and most likely in my case, public embarrassment.

I was one of the first kids to enter U.S. History class.

Unfortunately, that didn't mean I got to pick my own desk. Ms. Miller preferred assigned seating.

"Ms. May, your desk is over by the wall, fourth one back." Thankfully, Ms. Miller preferred addressing her student's more formally so I was able to avoid being called Chunky for at least forty minutes.

Plopping down into my seat I watched the door as other kids started to arrive. Butter walked in with Eric close on his heels. Several other girls I'd known for years but seldom spoke with, due to the fact that they were varsity cheerleaders and I wasn't, entered close behind the guys. I watched as they giggled and shimmied their way over into their seats.

Unfortunately, and far worse than the cheering squad, were Chad and a few of his buddies. I quickly looked down at my desk before he could catch me looking at him. I didn't know what was happening with Chad and this whole strange vibe thing he was putting off, but I was going to do my best to ignore it. Of course, I realized a few moments later, this was going to be a lot harder with him sitting right beside me.

"Well, if it isn't my great buddy, Chunky," Chad drawled. A few of his friends sitting close by, chuckled. Though I personally didn't get the joke, I halfheartedly smiled a hello over at him, before reaching for my bag, searching for my pen and paper.

Ms. Miller began talking about the class and all of her one hundred and one expectations of us. I noted that the desk behind me remained empty and I hoped fervently that that would be Dean's. A few minutes later, that was confirmed when Dean walked in with a late note and Ms. Miller pointed the desk behind me out to him.

Dean made his way over and down the row. He gave me a grin and a wink when he saw me. I heard Chad scoff a second later, and mumble something I didn't quite catch. I decided I probably wouldn't want to know anyway, and refused to look over at him again.

Class pretty much flew by after that. Though I could feel

Chad watching me a time or two, it was pretty easy to block him out. It was Dean sitting behind me that I found far more difficult to ignore.

When the bell finally rang to dismiss class I was more than ready to go. I needed some distance from Dean to get some serious perspective and a clear dose of reality.

Dean was only a step behind me as I walked out of the classroom. "What's your next class?"

Glancing back over my shoulder at him and up, way up, I answered. "I have algebra II with M..."

Before I could finish, Dean had wrapped his arm around my collarbone and was whipping me back into hard contact with his body.

"What in the wor..." I started to say, before I realized that Dean had seen what I hadn't; a couple of guys horsing around. They would have slammed right into me if Dean hadn't grabbed me so quickly and pulled me out of the way.

I stood there for a few minutes with my heart racing. I was ever so conscious of Dean's strong arm wrapped around me from behind, holding me protectively to him. His entire front was plastered to my back. It felt great. He felt great. Then in a split second I realized he could feel me too, and in my mind, that wasn't a good thing.

I took a quick step forward and away from him and quickly turned my body from further contact. "Wow! Quick reflexes," I attempted to joke while wondering frantically if he'd noticed just how plump I was while he held me in his arms.

"You okay?" he asked, looking at me with what appeared to be genuine concern. I looked at him closely. If he was feeling any disgust at having my chunky body pressed up against his, he was doing a great job of hiding it.

"I'm fine. Fine," I assured him as I shifted my book bag over to my other shoulder.

"Idiots," Dean mumbled, running his hand through his hair. "They should know better than to do that kind of crap in the hallways. There's barely enough room to walk let alone horse around in here."

"I'm fine. Really," I said, waving my hands and wiggling my fingers at him. "No harm no foul."

Dean huffed out a laugh at my antics as I'd hoped he would. The quicker he forgot about this, and I mean *all* of this, the better for my peace of mind.

"As I was saying before I was so *rudely* interrupted," I teased. "Was that I was heading to algebra II with Ms Baker. What about you?"

"Same," Dean said.

"Well then, shall we?" I asked, sweeping my arm out, palm up in an overly dramatic gesture.

"We shall," he answered, before placing his hand along his stomach and giving me a slight bow.

And like two very big idiots we made our way to class, talking with upper crust British accents about things of no consequence and very little substance. But it was fun.

5. Friendship

Sixth period dragged. Never a fan of algebra to begin with, the sequel looked as if it would be equally obnoxious. I tried my hardest to pay attention to what Ms. Baker was saying but my mind kept straying back to the hallway and Dean. I was finding that the protective clinch I had unexpectedly found myself in, no matter how innocently intended, was a hard thing to forget. Not only that, but everything that came after. I had almost acted like a completely different person.

Yeah, I played and joked around with Peanut or Butter—people I knew pretty well and who knew me, but I never, absolutely never, let my guard down around people that I didn't really know. Especially really hot strangers who made me melt with a look. Everything had felt so natural with Dean and he had seemed to feel it, too.

Then again, I asked myself, what did I know? I had about as much experience with guys today as I did five years ago. Maybe I was making too much out of this. It's obvious that Dean is a nice guy and nice guys would protect someone from getting hurt or goof off with them while walking to class. This was not the stuff epic romances are made of. Get a grip on yourself, Chunky girl. Stop reading more into things than what is there---and what is *not* there is romantic interest. Friendship interest, yes–probably--maybe but nothing more and the sooner I come to terms with that, the better off I'm going to be.

The bell ringing, drug me from my inner reflections. I stuffed my pencil, notebook, and dreaded new algebra II book into my book bag.

"See you later, Ch...," Dean started saying, before he hesitated for a quick second then simply repeated, "See you later," with an awkward little wave of his hand.

"Bye," I answered just as simply with a smile and quick wave. I watched as he walked off with a few of the football players. I smiled though I wasn't really sure why.

Swinging my now overly stuffed book bag over my shoulder, I started to walk to my locker. There was no reason I needed to carry everything home tonight. Only one class had given an assignment and that didn't require a book. I met Peanut along the way.

"Walk with me to my locker?" I asked, as she fell into step beside me.

"Sure," she answered. "Butter is giving me the keys to Princess so I can drive us home."

"No way?" I said with surprise. Butter loved that car and hated for anyone to drive it. "How did you manage to make that happen?"

Peanut grinned mischievously. "I told him I'd talk him up to Veronica Matton."

"Veronica? Butter likes Veronica?" I asked with shock. Butter's usual type was the flashy cheerleader pep girl type not the Veronica Matton, quiet brainy type. I mean, don't get me wrong. Veronica's great and I would say that she is one of my closest friends, but I'm flabbergasted that Butter has even noticed her other than to get help with homework. Which made me think...?

"He's not interested in her to use her, is he?" I asked with a frown. I loved Butter but I wasn't about to let him do something like that.

Peanut looked offended on her brother's behalf. "Geez Chunky, you know he wouldn't do that! Shame on you for even thinking he would."

"Sorry," I muttered feeling that shame. I had a feeling my reaction was based on my own personal insecurities rather than any real belief that Butter would be capable of acting that way. "I didn't mean it, Peanut. Of course, Butter wouldn't. I was just surprised to hear you name Veronica. I can't remember Butter ever talking about her. He's usually talking about Brooke and Heather and Emilee. I don't think I've ever heard him talk about Veronica. How did that happen?"

We reached my locker by this time and I was quickly unloading my books. It was a relief to get rid of the heavy load. My shoulder blades were killing me. So much for the law that stated students shouldn't carry home more than thirty pounds.

"Butter and I went to pick up dinner a couple of weeks ago at the little diner on First Street, Dixie Queen. Anyway, when we went inside, Veronica was there. She evidently started working there over the summer. You know how sweet she is, right?" Peanut asked, as we turned away from my locker and headed toward the parking lot. "Well, there was this rude customer who was giving her a really hard time about the size of the to-go cups or something really lame like that. He was being such a jerk that Veronica burst into tears. It really ticked Butter off. So he walked up to Veronica and put his arm around her like they were a couple and asked the customer if there was a problem. Seeing as how Butter is a giant and this guy wasn't, the customer shut up and walked out."

I looked at Peanut confused. "Then why do you have to talk to Veronica about Butter. It seems to me he already put a good word in for himself. I mean please, can you say freaking white knight in shining armor?"

Peanut giggled at me, and my description of her brother, before turning back to the conversation. "Actually what he did is kind of why I told him I'd talk to her. You see, her boss overheard the last half of the exchange between Butter and the customer and her boss thought Butter really was her boyfriend and that he was frightening off customers."

"Please don't tell me Veronica's boss fired her?" I groaned aloud.

"I always did say you were smart, Chunky. Yep. Her boss fired her on the spot and in front of the entire restaurant crowd. Needless to say it was pretty humiliating for her."

"And she blames, Butter," I guessed.

"And she blames, Butter," Peanut confirmed.

"Ouch!" I grimaced, hating it for Butter. If he was willing to put his sister up to putting a good word in for him he must really like this girl. Butter wasn't a heart-on-your sleeve kind of guy. Actually, some of the time, I thought he could be about as dim and uninteresting as Chad and his friends could be. It was nice to know under all that goofiness lurked a decent guy.

Peanut unlocked her car door then quickly hit the automatic button to unlock mine. We both climbed in simultaneously, slamming the heavy doors with loud thuds.

"What a day!" I said aloud, pushing the button so that the windows would go down. The late August weather in North Carolina was always a scorcher and today was no exception. As much as I loved the mild climate of Greenville, sometimes, like today for example, we had our fair share of extremes in temperature.

"You can say that again," Peanut agreed, before turning to look at me directly. "And when I say you, I do mean *you*. My goodness, Chunky you had quite the eventful first day, didn't you?"

I tried to look all innocent. "I really don't know what you're talking about."

"Yeah right," Peanut scoffed, turning her attention back to the front and pulling out of the parking space. "Let's skip over the boring parts like Mrs. Drysdale's weird bellowing of your name for the entire school to hear, and your falling on your face in first period. Let's go right to the good stuff, shall we. Namely Dean."

I felt my face heat and I didn't think it had anything to do with the temperature outside or inside the car. I knew this moment would come. From the moment since lunchtime when Peanut gave me her little 'call me' signal, I knew the third degree was coming. I just wasn't ready, which made everything even more uncomfortable for me because I could *always* talk to Peanut about *everything*. I had very few secrets from her. But this, this was different and I didn't know why.

"So what do you think of Dean?" she asked.

I was glad she had started with an easy one. "I like him."

Peanut whipped her face around to look at me, before turning her attention back to the road. "You're kidding me right? That's it? You know I was asking for a whole lot more than that."

Figures, I thought, smiling to myself. Nothing was ever easy. "What more do you want?"

"You do realize Chunky that you're telling me a lot simply by what you're *not* saying."

"Huh?" I questioned playing dumb.

"Okay Chunky, let's have it. What's going on?" Peanut demanded as she turned into my driveway and slammed the car into park.

I looked up at the house I had lived in my entire life. It was a simple home. There was nothing grandiose about it, but I loved it. It was a Cape Cod style home that sat in the middle of the yard with almost a dozen pine trees. Every year my Dad could be heard grumbling about having to rake the pine needles up but I've always thought that it was mostly an act. If anything, I think my dad is kind of proud of what he's built for us.

I sighed softly. So much history was behind those walls. So many laughs, tears and secrets shared. It seemed today would be no exception. Peanut was wanting some answers and truth be told, I was kind of looking forward to giving them to her, within reason, of course.

"So?" Peanut prompted in impatience. It was obvious that she felt she had waited long enough.

Rolling my eyes and seeing no reprieve in sight I gave in. "Let's go inside and get something cold to drink."

"And you'll tell me everything?" Peanut prompted.

"And I'll tell you everything."

A few minutes later, cold glasses of iced tea in our hands we headed up to my bedroom. Placing the tea where I felt it could do the least amount of damage if spilled, I plopped down onto my queen size bed, groaning and stretching, trying to release the tensions of the day.

"Okay, let's hear it," Peanut ordered while making herself comfortable on the giant plush pillow on my floor.

"Where do you want me to start?" I hedged.

"Tell me about Chad."

I sat up on the bed so fast I thought I had managed to give myself a case of whiplash. That was the very last thing I was expecting her to say. *I* knew that *she* knew he had been staring at me this morning because *I'm* the one who had pointed it out to *her*. But I hadn't realized that she knew there was any more to it than that. I thought that I had been the only one who had noticed Chad's bizarre behavior throughout the day, and I can guarantee you I hadn't planned on mentioning it to anyone. Not even by bringing it back up to Peanut.

"Chad? What about him?" I asked in an offhand manner. I still didn't plan on talking about it if I could help it.

"You tell me," Peanut answered right back with a determined jut to her chin. "And don't even say "what" again. *I'm* not budging until *you're* talking!"

I slowly lowered myself back down onto the bed, propping my head up with my hand under my chin. I knew when I was fighting a losing battle. "I really don't know what to tell you Peanut. He just acted really weird around me today."

"You mean like weird as in watching you like earlier this morning?"

"Yes, exactly like that." I answered with a worried frown. "You don't think anybody else noticed it do you? I really don't want there to be talk."

Peanut looked like she was considering my question before finally answering me. "No, I don't think so. Not really, at least not during lunch. Those idiots he was sitting with were busy throwing french fries at the cheerleaders. I probably wouldn't have noticed it myself if I hadn't been watching you."

"Why were you watching me?"

Peanut smiled. "Because I was trying to eavesdrop on your and Dean's conversation," she confessed.

"I can't believe you have the guts to admit that!"

"And I can't believe how hard you're trying to change the subject," she shot right back at me.

"It's embarrassing, Peanut. It's not like Chad was ogling me in a good way or anything. I swear I felt like he hated me but there was something else. And it seemed to get worse when he saw Dean sitting with me in the cafeteria. It's pretty obvious why he hates Dean, but I'm really not getting why he's hating on me. I mean, I haven't even seen him since the end of school last year and I can't think of anything that happened then that could be making him act like this. Not that he's acting like anything," I tried to clarify in my frustration. "He really hasn't done anything... much..." I finally stuttered to a stop. I wasn't explaining myself very well.

Peanut absentmindedly slipped off her shoes while watching me with an intense look on her face. I waited patiently to hear what was going on in that complex mind of hers. I didn't have to wait long.

"I guess technically, Chad hasn't done anything to you. But you're right to be weary. He's got this gleam in his eye when he looks at you and I don't trust it. Why he has it is anybody's guess. I would just be careful of him if I were you. I don't trust him."

"I've never trusted him, Peanut, and neither have you. It's probably something else and not really about me. As far as being careful around him, I plan on staying as far away from him as I usually do. That shouldn't be a problem."

Peanut nodded in agreement. "And if it looks like it's going to become a problem I'll have a little talk with Butter," she tacked on with another final nod to her head.

In the process of reaching for my glass of iced tea, my fingers almost knocked it over as I jerked in response to what Peanut had said. "No, Peanut," I instantly said. "Please no. That could get pretty embarrassing. The last thing I want is to bring this to the attention of other people. I could only imagine what kind of humiliating things Chad could come up with if given the opportunity."

Peanut looked at me with a thoughtful frown before finally agreeing not to tell Butter. "But!" she said holding up her index finger as if to emphasize her point. "If things get too far out of hand, the deals off and I tell Butter. Deal?" she asked.

"Deal," I agreed knowing I really didn't have any other choice.

"Now, back to Dean, Chunky," Peanut demanded. "What did you really think about him?"

I looked at Peanut sprawled out on the obnoxiously orange plush pillow that she had given me as a fifteenth birthday gift, waiting patiently for me to open up and be the best friend I had always been. Sharing secrets and confessing secrets was what we did best together and this would be no exception.

As if a weight had been lifted from me, I finally found the words to talk to my best friend and they weren't as hard to say out loud as I thought. "I think he could be someone really special to me," I confessed.

"He's pretty hot," Peanut chimed in.

"Oh yeah, he is," I agreed readily enough. "But that's only

a small part of it. He's sensitive, you know? He seems to know wrong from right and he's willing to stand up against the wrong because it's simply the right thing to do. That's amazing to me. And he's sweet and considerate and helpful and protective..."

"Wow!" Peanut said looking at me in amazement. "You learned all of that in just one day?"

I lowered my head in embarrassment at having been too obvious. "It wasn't all that difficult," I mumbled defensively. "We had three classes together plus lunch."

"Yeah, but you normally stay to yourself or with a couple of friends. And you definitely never hang out with a hot, new guy. Go Chunky!" Peanut cheered.

I rolled my eyes at her. There was no need to try and reason with Peanut when she got like this but, of course, I gave it a shot. "Come on, Peanut. We're talking about me—plump, klutzy me. Do you really think I stand a chance with someone like him over Emilee or Heather or one of those other girls?"

Suddenly all laughter left Peanut's face and she looked at me with total sincerity. "Yes, I do, Chunky. I really, really do. If Dean is even one-half the guy you described to me, then I most certainly do. It means he would be the kind of guy to recognize the treasure that is you. He'd be thrilled to have a girl on his arm with a little junk in her trunk and he sure as well would love being good to you, protecting you, appreciating *you*."

My eyes filled with tears as Peanut talked. I couldn't help myself. It was so nice having a friend see you the way you found it *impossible* to see yourself. "Peanut you are so sweet to say that but you really can't understand what it's like being like this. Not being the traditional girl and feeling uncomfortable in your own skin."

Peanut gave a short bark of laughter before she started shaking her head back and forth at me. "I don't understand, Chunky? *I* don't? Have you looked at me lately? I mean really looked. My mom is white Chunky and my dad is black. If anyone can understand not feeling comfortable in their own

45

skin sometimes it's me. I mean good lord I literally have *two* sets of skin I have to walk around in and sometimes its feels like neither of them fit."

Shocked beyond belief at my own self-centered attitude I immediately apologized. "I am such an idiot Peanut."

Peanut shook her head at me. "I'm not looking for an apology from you. One of the best things about you, Chunky, is that you don't see color. And believe it or not, I absolutely love that you are so blind to it that it takes me saying something like this for you to even see it. I was telling you this to make a point. No matter how good someone's life may appear on the outside, each and every one of us has things in our lives that make life a little more difficult."

"Yeah... well... uh," I stammered around. I was searching desperately around in my mind for something to say that would make me look less like a self-absorbed idiot. "You... umm... you made your point."

After a few seconds of staring at one another in silence we burst into a fit of teenage giggles. We were happy at that moment to be nothing more than girls.

6.   Girl Talk

Despite the exciting, chaotic and humiliating experiences of the first day, the rest of the week was somewhat anti-climatic. I experienced no other major catastrophe, which was really the highlight of the week for me. Dean still sat beside me at lunch and walked with me to fifth and sixth period, which was great but there wasn't anything more personal involved. We ate at the same time, so we sat together. We had the same classes at the same time, so we walked together. It was as simple and as uncomplicated as that.

As for Chad, he too, seemed to be acting more his usual self. I no longer experienced the chilling feeling that eyes were watching me and if we happened to make eye contact, which in U.S. History we usually did, due to seating arrangements, it was fleeting and uneventful. I'd have to say that was the second highlight of my week.

Of course it was only Thursday, I reminded myself, and a lot could happen in a day.

"Morning Dad," I said as I walked into the kitchen. I grabbed a clean glass down from the cabinet and poured myself a glass of orange juice.

"Morning Chunky," He answered giving me his habitual kiss on the cheek. "How's the new alarm clock working?"

I rolled my eyes at him saying without words that I didn't appreciate his attempt at humor. He chuckled in response. I turned my back to him to hide a grin. There was no need in encouraging his lame jokes.

Just as I swallowed the last bit of juice the sound of Butter's car horn signaled their arrival. It was later than I thought. "I gotta run. See you tonight and be careful!" I called over my shoulder. The word, "Always!" floated out to me before I shut the kitchen door.

In a few seconds I was inside the Honda Civic and we were backing out of the driveway. Peanut was already turned around in her seat and talking so fast I couldn't understand a word she was saying over the sound of Soulja Boy blaring through the speakers.

"What?" I yelled.

Peanut reached over and turned off the radio while completely ignoring Butter's bellow of outrage at having his favorite song cut short. "Did you hear about the big party this weekend?"

"No," I answered in some confusion. Peanut and I usually never went to "big parties" for a lot of reasons. Most of those reasons were that the people that *did* usually go to them weren't exactly our best friends. Chad instantly came to mind as an example.

"Everyone is going to be there. It's at Dean and David's. Have you met David yet?" she quickly asked, before launching into more rapture about the party before I could answer her one way or the other. "Anyway, they've invited pretty much all the junior and senior class. I hear their house is huge and they have a swimming pool. Their parents aren't going to be there, but they've okayed the party. Butter's going and Eric, Tammy, Shelly and even Veronica," she added, giving Butter a sly look.

"Shut up, Peanut!" he ordered half-joking and half-serious.

While they bickered back and forth I started to feel a little confused and hurt. If they had been planning this party all week then why was I just now hearing about it? Dean hadn't mentioned a word to me at all and we had talked every day.

"So you're going right?" Peanut asked, turning her attention back to me.

"I don't know," I answered slowly. My gut reaction was to say "heck no!" I mean, it wasn't like I was given an invite or anything.

Peanut looked back at me exasperated. "What do you mean you don't know?" she bellowed. "Of course you're going."

"How did you hear about this party?" I asked. I needed a little more detail before I committed to going to a party that I wasn't even sure if I was wanted.

"Butter," came Peanut's instant response. "He found out at practice last night. I guess it's a last minute thing but it's still supposed to be pretty huge."

I relaxed back in my seat after that explanation. The confusion and hurt slowly started to seep away. Unfortunately, that was quickly replaced by tension when I started to think about *actually* going to the party. I didn't do real well at parties. I often felt like the proverbial wallflower when I went to a party—which was why I usually elected not to.

"So we're going right?" Peanut kept nagging me from the front seat. "Of course, we're going," she answered herself.

"How's the team looking this year, Butter?" I asked. It was time to change the subject.

"Good. It's looking really good. Dean is an awesome quarterback. He's definitely better than Chad and that becomes more obvious every day at practice. I think the coach is going to play them both to start and let them battle it out on the field so to speak."

I winced at that. Chad wasn't going to be a good sport about it, of that I was sure. Things were going to get pretty tense for the team before they got better.

49

"Nobody is after your spot are they?" I teased him. Butter was good, real good, and he knew it. I liked to get him riled. It worked. The rest of the drive to school was a long-winded, ego- driven litany on the finer points of Butter the Baller. By the time he parked the car, Peanut and I were in tears from laughing so hard.

The first person I saw when I got out of the car was Dean and standing right next to him was a guy who couldn't be anyone else but David. Maybe a half an inch taller than Dean, David had the same looks right down to the dimples. Oh correction, I silently amended, one dimple.

They walked over toward us as we got out of the car. Dean, David and Butter did the jock fist to fist thing while Peanut and I looked on.

Dean turned toward us. "Hi guys! Have you met my brother, David?"

From David's casual greeting to Peanut, it became immediately apparent to me that Peanut and David had already met. I found this realization a little confusing since Peanut had yet to share this somewhat juicy tidbit with me. And that silence spoke a whole lot more loudly to me than mere words, which was something I would point out to her later when we were alone. As it was, I ignored the multitude of questions I was dying to ask Peanut, and instead I extended my hand to shake David's and murmured the nice pleasantries our parents taught us when we were young.

On closer inspection, I had to admit that David was definitely cute, but I couldn't help but think that Dean seemed to have a little something more that I couldn't put my finger on. He had something that made him stand out more than his brother. He had an 'IT' factor. And 'IT' made all the difference in the world.

We all turned to start walking toward school. David, Peanut and Butter walked a little further ahead while Dean walked with me. "Did Peanut tell you about our party?" Dean immediately asked me, destroying any lingering doubts I may have had about his not wanting me to be there.

"In the car this morning," I answered while fidgeting with the strap of my book bag.

"So, are you going to come?" he asked me with his hands outspread as if he'd been waiting for hours for an answer.

Crap, I thought to myself. I wanted to. I really did, but I was so afraid this party would turn out like every other party I'd ever been to. With me having the best of intentions to not just stand around but actively participate in conversations and dancing, only to have all of those intentions evaporate as I once again became the proverbial bump on the log.

"You don't have to come if you don't want to," Dean said, jamming his hands into the front pockets of his jeans. If I hadn't known any better I would have thought that he almost sounded a little hurt. But of course I knew that couldn't be true.

I quickly turned to look at him and noted that he seemed to be gritting his jaw and he wouldn't quite meet my eyes, which was funny really, because just a few moments before, *I* wouldn't meet his. I saw then that I *had* somehow hurt his feelings by taking so long to answer, which instantly made me feel horrible.

"No. No," I hurriedly started to speak. "Of course I'm coming. I'm catching a ride with Butter and Peanut." I silently said a prayer that I was making the right decision. If the relieved look on his face was anything to go by, then I was pretty sure I had.

Dean smiled really big. "That's great!" he said nodding his head and his eyes once again met mine with the habitual crystal blue twinkle I was so used to seeing.

I smiled back.

The bell rang at that moment and we quickly made our way to first period before the second bell could ring and mark us tardy. As luck would have it, or should I say lack of luck, I tripped on two separate occasions while we walked. Both times

Dean had to reach out and catch me to keep me from falling. By the time we reached the classroom my face was beet red. I couldn't help but wonder if *he* was starting to wonder if I was doing it on purpose. He didn't know me well enough yet, to know that that was just me being me.

Biology as usual was boring but at least Mr. Smith never gave out too much homework. While he droned on and on, I replayed the conversation I'd had with Dean in the parking lot. I had the feeling I'd be obsessing over this little encounter for the foreseeable future. He had seemed really upset when he thought I hadn't wanted to go to his party. He'd actually thought that I was trying to find some tactful way to say that I wasn't interested in attending a party that he was having. I couldn't help but feel flattered, especially after thinking only a short time ago that he hadn't even wanted me to be there at all. I smiled to myself. It was kind of cool being important to a hot guy like Dean, even if it was only in a platonic way.

I glanced over at him and about swallowed my tongue when I saw that *he* was staring at me with a little frown between his eyes. He quickly smoothed the frown away and flashed me his sweet grin, before turning his head and attention back toward Mr. Smith.

Curious and more curious, I thought to myself. What had all of that been about? Before I could reflect further Mr. Smith told us to turn our books to page twenty-two and I decided it was time that I started paying closer attention. Mr. Smith wasn't big on homework but I'd heard he was pretty big on pop quizzes. My dad would kill me if I brought home an F, not to mention he'd demand a good excuse for why I'd gotten it. I didn't think explaining that I was drooling over Dean would go over all too well with him.

The rest of the day flew by without anything unexpected happening. I didn't count almost stabbing myself in the hand with my newly sharpened pencil, because I was the only person who knew about it and it hadn't *actually* happened, so it didn't really count.

Peanut drove me home again. It was really the first chance I'd had alone with her since this morning's discovery that she'd met David Scott and not told me. I didn't hesitate to grill her.

"So when did you meet David and why didn't you tell me about it?" I verbally threw at her as soon as she pulled out of the school parking lot. I settled myself comfortably back against the door and awaited her reaction. It was her day to be in the hot seat.

The car lurched a little when Peanut lifted her foot off of the accelerator in an involuntary response to my question. After a half a beat she accelerated back up to the speed limit. I knew I was on to something.

"What do you mean?" she asked with innocence, but I wasn't fooled. I could see her unconsciously gripping the steering wheel tighter and her eyes kept darting little glances in my direction. I was the queen of pretending ignorance when I wanted to avoid a subject, Peanut however was not. She didn't stand a chance.

"Okay your turn. Spill it," I demanded. It was pretty unusual for Peanut not to tell me everything she was thinking and feeling. Whereas, I was the proverbial clam, Peanut was the canary.

Peanut glanced over at me, then back to the road before she somewhat reluctantly began to talk. "I saw him for the first time on Monday."

"At school?" I quizzed.

"No. I saw him at football practice. Remember my deal with Butter? I can drive the car after school but I have to pick him up after practice."

I nodded my head. "Oh yeah."

"Anyway, when I picked Butter up he was talking with a group of guys. Dean was one and when I saw the guy next to him, I knew it had to be David."

I laughed. "I know what you mean. I couldn't help but notice this morning how much they look alike." I glanced over at her. "Dean's hotter."

"I don't think so!" Peanut scoffed, whipping her neck back and forth punctuating each word as she spoke.

We both laughed.

"So..." I prompted her.

Peanut took a deep breath. "So, the next day when I went to pick up Butter, I tried to get there a little bit earlier. You know... hoping to see a little bit more of him. David," she quickly slotted in encase I misunderstood. "More of David, not Butter."

"No kidding," I responded with a roll of my eyes.

"Yeah, well my timing couldn't have been better because practice was still going except for David. I guess since he's the kicker he's not always needed for certain things. Anyway, he's nearing the entrance to the gym when I pull up and of course, I conveniently parked near the gym entrance. My timing, as usual was impeccable. I got out of the car and casually waved. I figured if he didn't remember me, no harm done. I'd just keep walking toward the field as if that had been my intention all along. If he did remember me and said anything, I could stop and chat."

"And which one was it?" I asked after a moment when Peanut didn't elaborate further.

"Neither, I guess. Or both," was her confusing answer.

"Sorry," I told her. "You're going to have to give me a little more than that."

I waited patiently for her explanation while she navigated a pretty harrowing curve. Eastern Carolina had a lot of flat land but some of the rural roads could be a bit tricky to drive on.

"He smiled at me, said 'Hi Peanut, Butter's over there' and continued to walk into the gym." She finally answered in a matter of fact tone once she had the car straightened back out.

I still didn't fully understand this conversation. It was pretty obvious Peanut had a bit of a crush on David, and believe me, I could fully understand how confusing and upsetting that could be. But what I couldn't understand was why she seemed so upset by this particular conversation. As far as I could tell, nothing bad was said. I mean yeah, it hadn't been the conversation of a life time, but the total dejection that I was sensing from her was confusing—combine that with her total secrecy about the entire David encounter and I was one confused chick.

"I'm sorry Peanut. I'm not trying to tease you or give you a hard time, but I'm really having trouble reading between the lines here."

A puff of laughter escaped Peanut as she dragged a tiny hand through her black hair. "You and me both," she said, before scrunching up her nose in concentration. "I can't really explain it to myself, Chunky, so it's kind of hard to explain it to you. David is... David, you know. When I met him it was... it was, well, different than any other time I've met a new guy. I felt like he looked at me you know. He talked to just me for a few minutes the first night we met, and as lame as this sounds, it felt like we'd made some sort of connection. I'm not saying it was something as cheesy as love at first sight or that I'm desperately in love, but it was something, you know. And the next day when I went to pick up Butter, but mostly to try to see David again, I felt so hopeful. So when he treated me like a little kid sister of one of his teammates, it cut kind of deep."

She pulled into my driveway and stopped the car, before turning to look at me. "Do I sound as lame as I think I sound?"

Considering she had just expressed exactly my own confusing thoughts where Dean was concerned, I wasn't about to answer yes. Instead I reached over and gave her a tight hug. "Those Scott boys are killers, huh?"

Peanut giggled, as I knew she would. "Is that an admission?" she asked.

I pulled back and winked at her. "Of a sort."

"We still going to the party tomorrow night?" she asked. She was not very successful in disguising the hope from her voice.

"Yeah, we're going," I answered halfheartedly as I got out of the car. I wasn't sure if it was the best idea in the world, but we'd go together. Surely the two of us could handle whatever came our way.

7. Getting Permission

Friday morning arrived with bright sunlight and clear Carolina blue skies. As I got ready for school I practiced telling my dad about tonight's party. The detective in him would ferret out any attempt at lies or embellishments, which meant I was stuck with telling the truth. And that was the problem. I wasn't too sure what he would think about a party with no parents.

A small part of me hoped he'd put his foot down and say absolutely not. That way I would have a legitimate excuse why I didn't go and no one's feelings would get hurt. The other part of me, the larger part, hoped he would say that it was okay. I was beginning to believe that tonight could be the start of that *different* I'd been talking about so much lately.

Taking a deep breath I started towards the kitchen. "Morning Daddy," I chirped sweetly while reaching for a glass to poor my habitual glass of orange juice.

"Oh no," he groaned in response. "You're breaking out the Daddy on me. What do you want?"

"I'm offended," I said, glaring at him to let him know I meant business.

Dad only laughed. "And I'm not a bit fooled, so cut out the act and let's have it."

"Okay," I said, before taking a deep breath and rushing

into speech. "There's a party tonight over in the South Hall neighborhood. It's being given by these two new guys who are brothers. They both play football and it's kind of a go Wolverines, slash hi we're new to town, kind of party. Their parents know about the party but they won't be there. Can I go?"

My dad stared at me for a few minutes without blinking.

"Dad?" I prompted when he still didn't say anything.

He held his hand up at me. "Give me a minute," he said. "My brain is still trying to process and decipher that sixty mile an hour drive by speech."

I took a sip of my juice and stared out the window, giving him his time. I knew this meant he was stewing it over. Though he wasn't saying no, I had the feeling it was his gut reaction---and my dad usually went with his gut. I started to lose some of my excitement.

"The parents know about the party?" he finally asked, while popping two pieces of bread into the toaster.

"Yes."

He placed his hands down flat onto the kitchen island and leaned in towards me with a stern look on his face, "Will there be any drinking at this party?" he asked in a tone that made it clear he had no time for any fabrications.

I frowned at him. "I honestly don't know. From what I know of Dean and David, I would have to say I wouldn't think so, but I'm not one hundred percent sure. If it helps, I have no desire to drink if there is," I freely and truthfully offered.

"It helps, but not much," he replied, pushing off from the island and reaching for the toast that had just popped up. "I trust you. It's the teenage idiots that drink themselves stupid, that I don't trust," he explained as he smothered his toast in butter and raspberry jam.

"What if I promise to leave if it appears that the party is getting out of hand?" I asked. "Butter is taking Peanut and me, if you let me go. You know he wouldn't let us stay if it got crazy."

I could tell my dad liked that answer. He was nodding his head in consideration while he chewed his breakfast. It wasn't that my dad was so sure Butter wasn't above a little drinking and partying. He just knew that there was no way Butter would let Peanut, or me for that matter, do the same. The male/female double standard still ran deep in the South.

"Do you know these boys? Have you actually met them and talked with them?" he asked around another bite of food.

I thought that was a strange question and said so. "What does that have to do with anything?"

He swallowed, before answering. "Because I want your honest opinion about them before I make up my mind and you can only give me that if you've spent time with them."

Man my dad was good.

"I've met David once. He's a senior and a kicker on the football team. He was very polite but that's all I know. But I have three classes with Dean and I usually sit beside him at lunch. He has good table manners, appears to have morals, seems pretty protective of the defenseless, plays quarterback and has a killer smile."

My dad stopped swiping at the crumbs on the countertop and looked over at me with a grin me. "Man, my daughter's good."

I burst into laughter.

"Quarterback, huh?" he asked. "I thought Chad was the quarterback?"

"So did Chad," I said with a grimace. "Coach plans to use both of them the first couple of games and I guess whoever does the best gets to start."

"Who's better?"

"Dean," I answered promptly.

"Killer smile, huh?" Dad asked with a grimace and a somewhat viscous last swipe of the counter.

Crap, I thought. Why had I said that? I gulped down my juice so I wouldn't have to answer. I refused to get into an in depth conversation with my dad about Dean and all his great attributes.

"Okay, you can go but I have some ground rules," he said, once he had stopped twisting and twisting the poor kitchen towel.

"Okay," I immediately agreed as I rinsed out my glass in the sink.

"First, there is to be absolutely no drinking and no riding in a car with someone drinking. If Butter drinks then either you or Peanut drive you guys home. If for some reason that doesn't get it, you call me and I'll pick you up. Deal?"

"Deal," I immediately agreed again while drying my hands on a towel.

"Second, I want you home no later than eleven-thirty. If Butter doesn't want to leave, you call me and I'll come and pick you up. No catching a ride with any friend. You won't be able to know everyone who drank or not and I don't want you taking any chances. Agreed?"

"Yes."

"Third, if at any time you become uncomfortable or you feel that there is something, *anything* not quite right, I want you to come home. If Butter doesn't want to leave, then you call me. Deal?"

"Yes!"

Dad closed his eyes and ran his hand over his face in a weary gesture. "You're going to turn me grey, Chunky girl," he sighed.

I laughed. "That's okay Dad, you're bald. It will be our little secret. No one will ever need to know." I leaned over to kiss him on the area under discussion, before making my way to the kitchen door. "You be careful!" I yelled.

"Always!"

I ran out to meet Butter and Peanut with a huge grin on my face.

"You can go!" Peanut guessed as soon as I was settled in the back seat.

"Yeah, can you believe it?" I asked. I was still a little shocked that my dad had actually agreed. "He had some ground rules, though," I clarified as I snapped the seatbelt into place.

"Like?" Peanut asked, turning around in her seat to look at me.

"The usual. No getting in a car with anyone drinking. If I feel like something isn't right to leave immediately. The usual police detective dad with a teenage daughter kind of rules," I added offhandedly.

Peanut giggled. She knew my dad all too well.

"So what are you planning to wear?" Peanut asked.

This elicited a long drawn out groan from Butter. I laughed. Butter hated silly girl talk. His words, not mine.

Of course my laughter only lasted a second when I realized I didn't have a clue as to what I would wear. "I don't know. What about you?"

"I've got it narrowed down to two outfits. My pink mini with the white and pink tank top or the butter yellow jean shorts with the yellow spaghetti strap top. Which one should I pick?"

"Wear the yellow one. Definitely the yellow one. That's your best color."

"So?" Peanut prompted. "What about you?"

"I'm going to have to give that some thought and get back to you. I spent most of last night and this morning trying to figure out how to ask my dad if I could go. I didn't give what I was going to wear a thought, though I can already tell you it won't be shorts."

"Why not?"

"Because," I answered, flashing my eyes to the back of Butter's head to indicate I didn't want to discuss this particular subject in front of him.

Unfortunately though, I didn't realize Butter was watching

me from the rearview mirror. "Leave her alone, Peanut. She's *sensitive*," he teased.

Peanut giggled as I popped Butter on the back of the head. There was no doubt that Butter knew all of my insecurities, but it didn't mean I *ever* wanted to talk with *him* about them. I did one-hundred-percent trust him not to disclose them, which was why I wasn't the least bit upset about what he'd said. It was the truth after all. I am sensitive. I can't help it. He just had the bad taste to throw it in my face because he was a Neanderthal. One who deserved a little pay back?

My lips twisted into a wicked grin and I gave Peanut a quick wink. "You know, it's a good thing that I *am* so sensitive, Butter." I innocently remarked.

Butter frowned at me in the rearview mirror. "What's that supposed to mean?" he asked, obviously and correctly sensing a trap.

"Well... I'm just saying," I drawled out while trying to maintain my innocent expression. "If I wasn't so *sensitive*, I'd probably tell everybody at the party tonight about how hard you cried when Old Yeller died."

"Ah!" Butter yelled, while Peanut giggled from the front passenger seat. "I was five years old when that happened!"

I started laughing, too. Any semblance of innocence was quickly wiped away at the chance of giving Butter a taste of his own medicine. "That's not the way I remember it!" I responded, before turning to Peanut and encouraging her to join in on the fun. "What about you, Peanut? Is that how you remember it?"

"What you're saying sounds real familiar, Chunky, really familiar. Didn't we just watch that the week before school started?" Peanut quizzed with her own brand of mock innocence.

"Hah! Hah!" Butter growled while turning the car onto the street where our school was. "We watched it years ago!"

"I'm just saying," I tried to explain with false sincerity, barely able to contain my triumphant grin. "When I tell everyone at the party tonight about your major meltdown when the doggie died, I might accidently leave *that* part of the story out. By accident," I then clarified just in case he wasn't catching on.

"Fine," Butter groaned in defeat as he turned the car into the school parking lot. "If that's the way you want to play it then, fine! You're not sensitive, Chunky. Not a bit. As a matter of fact, you're a barracuda; very mean and vicious. And as for you," he said with a distasteful glance in Peanut's direction, "Some sister you are."

Peanut and I dissolved into serious giggles at the very hard, put upon face Butter was striving to maintain before he, too gave into the stupidity of our conversation and started chuckling while shaking his head at us.

"This conversation doesn't go any further than this car," Butter warned, before pulling into what I was beginning to think of as "our" parking spot. "I have a reputation to uphold," he added then put the car in park.

In seconds we were out of the car and walking towards the quad. I saw Dean immediately. The fact that he was standing with Emilee and no one else made my stomach dip. She was smiling up at him and her hand was resting on his arm. Dean was flashing that stunning grin as he looked down at her, and he sure as heck wasn't throwing her hand off of his arm. Though I hadn't heard any gossip about these two, the scene looked very intimate to me. My excitement about tonight began to wane, and any remaining humor from the last few moments quickly disappeared.

Before anyone could catch me staring, I looked up at Butter and struck up a halfhearted conversation about football. Though I really wasn't interested, I knew it would get him going and I really needed some sort of a distraction. As he talked and we walked, we met up with Eric and Tammy and some of our other friends. Of course, the football conversation carried on, and I stood in the group seeming to be a part of it but very much apart from it.

I kept chastising myself for being so upset. Dean and I were just friends. He hadn't done anything wrong and neither had Emilee, but the urge to slap her and confront him was there nonetheless. It was just as if he really was my boyfriend and I had caught them sneaking around.

"Hey! What's up!" the object of my thoughts asked from over my shoulder. So caught up in my own thoughts that I hadn't heard him approach, I jumped a mile so that I knocked his chin with the top of my head and yelped out a piercing screech.

Everyone stopped talking at once and turned to stare at us. Mortified I could only stand there rubbing the top of my head while Dean grabbed at his jaw in obvious pain.

"Damn Chunky!" Chad called out suddenly into the awkward silence, drawing everyone's attention to him. "Maybe you should join the football team. You obviously have the strength and... Shall we say size, to sack the wannabe quarterback," he finished insinuatingly, eliciting several chuckles from around the quad, before walking off with his friends.

"Hey!" Butter said starting to walk after Chad but I quickly grabbed his arm to hold him back and was thankful Peanut helped me by grabbing his other one.

"Don't Butter," I pleaded. "He's not worth it and if you get caught fighting you'll get suspended from school and you won't be able to play football for three weeks." Peanut joined in and between the two of us he calmed down.

While all of this went on I couldn't help but notice that Dean was trying somewhat successfully to stop the bleeding from inside his mouth. The impact of my head must have made him split his lip. I also couldn't help but notice how Emilee was unsuccessfully trying to help him. It appeared that she didn't do all that well at the sight of blood.

The bell rang suddenly, interrupting everyone's overly excited recount of the last few minutes. I myself wanted to roll up into a ball and hide under a rock. I couldn't believe that

I'd not only almost given Dean a concussion but that Chad had said what he had. And the fact that half of the school had witnessed it made everything even worse.

As much as I didn't want to, I walked over to Dean. "Are you okay?" I asked. Digging inside my purse I pulled out a clean tissue. "Here, let me see," I ordered.

Lightly grabbing his jaw, I pulled his lower lip down with the tissue to inspect the cut, all the while apologizing a mile a minute. "I am so sorry. You startled me and I jumped. I don't know if you've noticed or not, but I'm kind of klutzy sometimes and well... if you're not careful around me you can become a casualty of my klutziness," I finished abruptly and somewhat lamely.

I also realized that I was still holding Dean by the chin and I quickly released him and took a step back. Of course I tripped over Dean's book bag that he had let fall to the ground when I'd almost knocked him unconscious. My arms started flailing as I tried to keep my balance, but I could feel myself falling anyway. That is until Dean reached out and grabbed my hands, pulling me into his arms and hugging me. It took me a second to appreciate exactly where I was and another split second to realize that the rumbling motion under my cheek was Dean's silent laughter.

"Oh, I've noticed," he said, still chuckling before he released me. He took a step back and palmed his jaw, giving a slight wince. "I've noticed," he repeated with a last chuckle and a wink. Bending over he picked up his book bag. "Let's go or we'll be late for Biology," he added and after the slightest hesitation on my part we started walking to class.

8. Ignoring Chad

Considering how bad the morning started, the rest of the day passed pretty quickly and harmlessly except for a few tense moments. One came in U.S. History. It was the first time I'd seen Chad and I could tell by the gleam in his eyes, he had a few more things to say. Fortunately, Mrs. Drysdale paged me to come to the library to help her with her art project and I was saved. I never thought I would be so happy to help Mrs. Drysdale as I was today.

The second uncomfortable moment came at lunchtime. Heather, Emilee and the rest of the cheerleaders were talking about this morning and as our table is next to theirs, everyone couldn't help but overhear. Everyone especially heard the part where Emilee kept going on and on about how bad it was of Chad to say what he did. Of course, the giggles she kept trying to disguise with her hand belied how *bad* she really thought it was of him.

Everyone at our table pretended not to hear it but I could and I knew they could. It was a bit of a struggle to get through the rest of lunch. If Peanut had not given me a little kick under the table and her patented Peanut glare, there was a really good chance that I might have run off crying. But I persevered, and though lunch lasted about five hours, or so it seemed, I made it through.

The hardest part was sitting beside Dean and trying to act normal. I could talk about and pretend platonic friendship all day long but the truth was he was working his way into my heart and having him be a witness to Chad's fat joke at my expense wasn't exactly easy to ignore. Add Emilee's catty rehashing of the entire episode to the actual event and you got a recipe for agony.

Thankfully though, lunch did finally end. Dean gathered our trash together as had become his habit and walked away to throw it into the garbage can.

"You okay?" Peanut whispered.

"Do I have a choice?" was my somber reply.

"I wish we would have let Butter clobber him earlier."

I huffed out a laugh. "No you don't. Just think how insufferable Butter would have become after three weeks of no football," I reminded her.

"Good point," she quickly agreed. "Still, I don't want him to get away with it."

"Let it go Peanut," I told her. "There will always be Chad or someone like Chad to hate on the horizontally challenged. You can't let yourself get worked up every time you overhear someone make a fat joke."

"But you're not fat!" she snarled.

"Shhh," I told her as I glanced over my shoulder. "Dean is coming back."

Peanut looked mutinous. "Well, I bet if we asked him he would agree with me!"

I turned to Peanut with my finger pointed at her. "Don't you dare!" I warned her. "Don't you dare or I'll..."

"You'll what?" she asked, looking very interested.

"I don't know but it will be bad. I can promise you that," I responded trying to sound as threatening as I could.

"Of course I won't Chunky, but God you drive me crazy

sometimes. Did you ever stop to consider that just because Chad said it, doesn't make it true?"

I shook my head at Peanut. We'd had this argument too many times to count and it was pretty obvious we would never agree. "I have a mirror Peanut and it tells me everything I need to know."

"Maybe you need to get a new mirror," was her parting shot. And with a toss of her head and her tiny nose in the air, she flounced off to her fifth period class in a total Peanut snit.

"Yeah," I mumbled to myself as I watched her walk away. "That will fix everything."

"What did you say?" Dean asked from beside me.

"Um… nothing. Just talking to myself," I said without meeting his eyes. Of course, on top of everything else, he had to catch me talking to myself.

"Talking to yourself is the first sign of insanity, they say," Dean teased.

His teasing made me smile on the inside. "Oh… I think it's too late to worry about that," I murmured, swinging my book bag over my shoulder.

"Crazy, huh?" Dean asked with a smile.

I cocked my head at him and finally smiled back, a real smile. Dean just had that kind of effect on me. "Don't forget klutzy. That's Crazy Klutzy Chunky to you," I found myself teasing him back, whereas just moments before, with Peanut, I had been all caught up in my old insecurities.

Dean's laughter drew my attention back to him. We started walking towards class when I heard him quietly murmur, "Oh I won't forget. I could never forget."

I snuck a look up at him from under my lashes but his face revealed nothing but good humor. And his good humor had wrapped itself around me, allowing the last few minutes with Peanut to wash away.

The rest of the day flew by. I spent the majority of it regretting my decision to go to this party tonight. After this morning's fiasco, the last thing I wanted to do was hang out with all of the witnesses to my humiliation. They'd either be laughing at me to my face, laughing at me behind my back or worse, feeling sorry for me. None of those three things were conducive to a fun night in my opinion.

The bell rang signaling that we were free until Monday. I swung my book bag over my shoulder and stood up.

"See you tonight?" Dean asked more than stated. It appeared he was starting to know me pretty well.

Well, I'd show him he didn't know me as well as he thought he did. "Of course. I already told you I was going." I had no problem pretending that I hadn't been thinking of a hundred different excuses to get out of going.

Dean's dimples flashed at me. "Just making sure," he said innocently. I had the feeling I hadn't fooled him in the least.

Dag gone it, I thought as I walked to my locker. Now I had to go to the party. I sure showed him, I silently and sarcastically mocked myself.

As had become ritual, Peanut met me on the way. "Decided on what you're going to wear tonight?" she asked. It was obvious that she'd decided to ignore everything except what she wanted and what she wanted was for me to go to this stupid party tonight. Between her and Dean, I didn't stand a chance.

"Not yet," I mumbled in an ungracious surrender.

Peanut ignored my gloom and doom and focused on the one good part. I was going.

The drive home was made in silence and when I say silence I mean without us talking, because the car itself wasn't silent. Beyoncé, Peanut's current favorite, was singing at the top of her lungs.

"Want me to come inside and help you pick out something to wear?" Peanut asked, as she pulled into my driveway and braked to a stop.

"Nah," I answered. "Besides, I already have a couple of ideas."

"And they would be?" Peanut asked with skepticism.

"Um... well... jeans or jeans," I answered in my best Paris Hilton imitation.

"Chunky..." Peanut started to warn but I cut her off. She wanted me to go and I would go. But I wasn't exactly looking forward to it and clothes were really the last thing on my mind.

"I won't embarrass you," I told her. "And I'll be presentable. Take it or leave it."

Peanut gave me a long considering look out of the side of her eye. "I'll take it," she finally decided. "We'll pick you up at eight."

"Okay," I said. "See you later," I called over my shoulder as I climbed out of the car and headed inside, going straight to my bedroom.

Throwing my book bag onto the floor I walked over to my closet and opened the double doors with gusto. Funnily enough, I really did have a pretty good idea of what I was going to wear tonight. I had a pair of Old Navy cargo pants that could pass for casual with a new top Peanut had recently talked me into buying on a shopping trip. The top was a light rose color that nipped in at the waist but it wasn't too short that it showed my belly. It had a big, scooped neck so that it subtly hung off of one shoulder. I'd have to wear my white strapless bra with it so no strap would show. I briefly contemplated (and by briefly I mean for a nanosecond) going braless. But I knew that there was no way I could get away with that with the size of my chest. As liberating as I'm sure going braless was, I just wasn't made that way; literally or figuratively.

Flopping down onto the bed I closed my eyes and let out a tired sigh. I wish I were the kind of girl who could wear one of those tiny petite shorts outfits like Peanut. They looked so casual yet so stylish at the same time. But when on me... well... not so much.

Yawning, I rolled over onto my side and found myself

drifting off to sleep. The next thing I knew I heard the kitchen door slam shut. I glanced over at my new alarm clock and noted that it was almost six. I had slept for about three hours. I couldn't believe it. I never took naps. Today must have been more mentally exhausting than I realized.

I extended my arms and legs out one at a time, enjoying the stretching sensation. I felt completely refreshed which was good because I needed all the advantages that I could get if I was going to get through tonight.

"Chunky?" my dad's booming voice called from the hallway. I could hear his heavy footsteps getting closer and closer. "Chunky?" he said again, giving my bedroom door a light tap before walking in. "Were you sleeping?" he asked with shock.

I grinned at him sheepishly. "Yes. It surprised me too."

"Are you feeling okay?" He asked, as he walked over to me and put his palm on my forehead. "You're not warm."

"I'm fine, Dad," I said, pulling away from his hand. "Just fell asleep, I guess." There was no way I was going to tell him that I had fallen into some kind of exhausted slumber due to mental overload.

"You feel okay enough to go to this party tonight?" he asked, not trying to disguise in the least the hopeful note in his voice that I would say no.

"Nice try. I'm still going."

Dad frowned down at me. "You don't sound real excited about it."

I wasn't but he didn't need to know that. It looked like operation fake your way through it started now. "Oh no, I am. Just still a little groggy from my nap," I explained.

He stared down at me a little bit more before finally nodding his head and walking back to the door. "Why don't you go and take a shower. It will help wake you up."

"Good idea," I said as cheerfully as I could. "I think I'll do that."

"Okay and I'll put some burgers on the grill while you do that so it should be ready by the time you're dressed."

"That sounds great!" I said feeling and quite possibly sounding like Tony the Tiger. Twenty minutes later. I was out of the shower and wearing an old t-shirt and shorts. I didn't want to get dressed for the party until after I ate. My hair was combed out and I was leaving it to mostly air dry. I'd style it after I got dressed. The makeup and other last minute touches would wait till then too.

"Smells good," I commented as I walked into the kitchen. "Want to eat outside on the patio?"

"Sure," my dad agreed. "We should take advantage of this great weather while we still have it. I'll grab the plates and you get the glasses."

"Chips or potato salad?" I asked him as he started to walk outside.

"Both," he answered with a laugh. "I'm starved."

Giggling, I grabbed the chips, potato salad, ketchup, mustard and pickles and made my way very carefully to the back door. "Dad!" I yelled for help.

In seconds he was there and between the two of us we had the food laid out and glasses filled. "Buns!" I said laughing. Jumping up I ran back into the kitchen and grabbed the hamburger buns from the bread cabinet. "Can't have my dad eating bunless hamburgers," I said jokingly, as I came back outside and laid the buns on the table. Dad laughed at my playfulness as he reached for one of the previously missing buns.

Looking over at him I felt really good for the first time that day. Who knew what would happen tonight at the party. It could be okay or it could really suck. Either way, I still had right now, and right now was pretty darn great.

9. Splash of the Party

A few minutes before eight I was as ready as I would ever be. My hair did exactly what I wanted it to for a change which had to be a good omen. It never did what I wanted it to. Standing in front of the full, length mirror I double checked my makeup—not that I wore that much. Turning right then left I gave myself a thorough once over before feeling satisfied with the final result.

"They're here!" Dad called.

Closing my eyes and taking a deep breath I turned away from the mirror, stuffed my money and license into my back pocket and walked out of my bedroom.

"Bye, Dad," I said placing a quick kiss on his cheek as I passed by him.

"Bye," he answered. "Have fun and *you* be careful!" he yelled at my departing back.

I grinned. "Always!"

Warm air hit me as I walked outside. It was a great night for a party. I waved at Butter and Peanut as I approached the car.

"You look great," Peanut approved as soon as I got in. "That rose color is perfect with your skin tone. And nice shoes. I don't remember seeing them before," she said as she craned around in her seat to get a better look at my feet.

"Thanks," I said, holding my leg up so she could stop twisting herself into a pretzel just so that she could see a pair of matching, rose, rhinestone encrusted mini slip on heels.

"You look great, too," I finally offered once the shoe inspection was over. "I told you yellow was a perfect color on you."

"Thanks," Peanut preened, smoothing invisible wrinkles from the soft material "What do you think of Butter?" Peanut asked.

I scooted up into the middle of the back seat to peer around at him. I felt my jaw drop. Butter was a Baller but this Butter was a player. "Oh. My. Gosh," I said in amazement. "You look freaking fantastic!" Instead of baggy shorts, a t-shirt and flip flops, Butter was wearing a pair of khaki slacks with a red polo shirt that clung to a rather impressive chest.

Butter looked pleased by my reaction. "Good answer," he said.

"I take it this isn't for my benefit, but for Veronica's?" I mused with a teasing smile.

"Very funny," he said, starting the car and backing out of the driveway.

"You wound me, Butter," I continued. "My heart is breaking and you don't even care," I whined in a pitiful voice, throwing my wrist across my eyes in classic tragic heroine style.

"You want me to drop you off right here?" Butter threatened.

Peanut and I laughed. It wasn't very often that we got the opportunity to embarrass Butter so we had to take complete advantage when we got the chance. Right now was one of those times. Knowing Butter was dressing up to impress some girl and that there was no way for him to deny it was too good to be true. Peanut and I did our best to turn Butter the color of his shirt for the rest of the drive to South Hall.

"Oh my God!" Peanut suddenly said. "Look at all the cars! This party is going to be huge."

I stared out my side of the car. The driveway and surrounding streets looked as bad as school. Thankfully, Butter's little hatchback was so small he was able to squeeze into a tiny spot not too far away.

Dean and David's house was huge. I knew it was going to be nice because all the homes in South Hall were, but I hadn't realized it was going to be one of the better ones. The yard was immaculately pruned and enormous. The driveway was at least three times the length of mine. For the first time I started wondering about Dean and David's parents and what they did for a living. It was clear they didn't work at the police department.

Music could be heard coming from the back of the house. Lights glowed from every window. Silhouettes of people could be seen in almost every room. "Wow," I whispered to Peanut.

"Double wow," she whispered back.

"Why are you two idiots whispering?" Butter asked from behind us where we had stopped dead in our tracks to take everything in.

We looked at each other and shrugged before breaking into laughter.

"Come on," Butter urged in a disgusted tone that reflected quite clearly his inability to understand the inexplicable silliness of girls.

The three of us walked up the long driveway toward the house.

"Front or back?" Butter asked. At the same time the front door opened and David appeared waving at us. "Front it is, then," Butter answered for himself.

"You okay?" I whispered to Peanut.

"I think so," she whispered back.

After that there wasn't any time for whispering because David had walked down the sidewalk to meet us.

"Hey guys, glad you could come!"

We all smiled our thanks and said our hellos. David shepherded us through the front doors and into the house.

"Come on this way," he called over his shoulder and we followed him through a maze of rooms, one seeming more impressive than the other. Each room was packed with loud teenagers, some I recognized and some I didn't.

We ended up in a pretty impressive game room. There was a pool table, foosball table, play station 3 and a multitude of other complicated looking gadgets that would appeal to most guys.

"Dag, this is nice," Butter said as he looked around.

"Thanks," Dean said suddenly appearing from behind me, startling me at the unexpectedness of it.

"Careful there," Dean laughed, putting his hands on my shoulders as if to hold me down. "My jaw still hasn't recovered from earlier."

Everyone around us laughed. I could feel my cheeks turn red but I bluffed my way through with a show of bravado.

"Well then, you should make sure to watch out where you put your jaw from now on," I warned.

Everyone laughed again and any tension I had been feeling began to seep away only to sky rocket back up when Dean leaned down over me from behind with his hands still warm on my shoulders to whisper in my ear, "I think I'm going to have to keep my eye on you. I'm starting to think that you're trouble."

His warm breath on my ear and neck tickled in a surprisingly good way. I struggled for a witty comeback but it was difficult. "I'll try to behave myself tonight," was the best thing I could come up with.

A puff of laughter escaped Dean's lips and it was all I could do to not physically react to the warm air as it caressed my neck, but Good Lord it felt good.

"Ahh," he groaned out loud. "Duty calls," he indicated with a sweep of his hand to more new arrivals and calls for more drinks.

"Go... go," Peanut urged with a smile on her face. "We'll be fine."

With a last smile Dean walked away. We watched as he was swallowed up by the crowd. I found myself admiring his tall, lean frame encased in faded denim and white polo shirt.

"Do you guys see Veronica anywhere?" Butter asked, craning his neck all around.

I drew my eyes away from Dean's disappearing figure to look at Butter and shook my head no. So did Peanut. "I'm going to look around," he told us and we nodded our understanding as he started out of the room.

"Wow Chunky!" Peanut immediately started. "I think Dean is flirting with you."

"Don't start that Peanut. He's just being nice"

Peanut shook her head at me. "No Chunky. I'm dead serious. I think Dean is flirting with you. I'm not saying he's about to ask you out on a romantic date, but the boy is definitely flirting."

"And I'm totally crushing on him Peanut so please, please don't encourage me. I need absolutely no help from you in that particular direction. What I do need is for you to say that he's a nice guy Chunky, but don't read anything else into it. You'll only get your heart broken if you do."

Peanut rolled her eyes at me. "Okay," she agreed. "Don't blah blah blah. Blah blah blah."

I laughed out loud. "Peanut, I'm serious!"

"And so am I!" Peanut laughed back. "Come on, let's walk around and check this place out some more. I'm not too interested in the games but I would like to see if we can find Veronica if Butter hasn't already. I feel the need for a little matchmaking tonight," she grinned wickedly at me.

I held my hands up with palms out in surrender. "That sounds good to me just as long as your matchmaking involves only Butter and Veronica and not me."

Peanut gave a wicked chuckle. "My matchmaking always includes you, Chunky girl. Always."

"Come on," I said, grabbing her arm and heading in the opposite direction Butter had gone.

We must have walked around for about fifteen minutes with no sign of Butter or Veronica. No sign of Dean either, I noted.

"Let's get something to drink," Peanut suggested.

I couldn't argue with that. Several rooms were set up with refreshments and we each grabbed a soda. I'd noticed earlier that some people were drinking beer but I had a feeling they hadn't gotten the beer from here. I'd yet to see one bar or anything alcoholic on offer.

Peanut and I stopped and chatted several times with different people for the next hour. We would periodically run into David or Dean but they never stayed to chat for long. Peanut and I both hid our disappointment with that pretty well. As hosts of the party, they had a duty to circulate and take care of their guests. It wasn't their fault that we were there mostly for them.

A while later, as we made our way into another room I finally asked Peanut about David. "I noticed David met us outside tonight when we got here. Was he just being nice or could he have possibly been on the lookout for you?" I quizzed.

"I don't know, Chunky," Peanut said in frustration. "I feel like I'm in the same boat as you. Maybe I'm just thinking something's there when there's not. Maybe I'm making more of something than it is. I did think he might have been waiting for me earlier, but now that I've only seen him a handful of minutes since we got here almost two hours ago, I'm not so sure."

Considering I could say the exact same thing about Dean, I really didn't know what I could say to make her feel better. "My perspective is shot when it comes to the Scott brothers," I offered in sympathy making Peanut giggle which was what I had intended.

"Let's go outside and check out the pool," I suggested. "The front yard is so gorgeous I can't imagine what the back looks like."

"Okay," Peanut agreed. "But I need to use the bathroom first. Where is it?"

"I went to the little half-bath right off the front entrance."

"Okay. I'll only be a minute."

"I'm going to go ahead and go out the back. It's getting a little stuffy in here."

Peanut nodded her understanding. "See you in a little bit and remember," she teased. "Stay out of trouble."

I was smiling as I made my way through the throng of guests. I would have to say that Dean and David's party was a success. Despite being the new kids on the block, at least half of the junior and senior classes were here. David and Dean were not going to have any difficulty fitting into Mansfield High, I thought, as I walked out the backdoor and into a paradise.

The backyard was massive with professional landscaping that made it a private oasis. The pool was kidney shaped with selective lighting and the water appeared crystal clear with a sea blue lining. A hot tub sat off to the side of the pool, connected yet separate. Bubbles frothed within the small circle that would seat about six people, though it sat empty now. Flowers and plants in varying colors, shapes and sizes abounded. It was sultry and enveloped the senses. Whoever had designed this was a true artist.

My feet were on automatic pilot as I walked along the edge of the pool. Nobody was currently swimming but a few people sat on the edges with their feet dangling in the water while they talked. Instinctively I walked away from these groups and further towards the end of the pool furthest away from the house. It seemed more secluded there and that appealed to me.

After a few moments of peace and quiet, I turned and started walking back the way I had come. Peanut had still not put in an appearance and I decided it was time to find her. A dark shadow moved beside me and stopped suddenly in front of me. Startled, I jumped, putting my hand to my throat.

A deep chuckle sounded from above my head. The chuckle didn't make me relax one bit. It didn't reassure me in the slightest. If anything, my heart started racing a little bit faster.

A hand reached out in the dark and grabbed the one I had placed at my throat. "What's the matter, Chunky?" Chad said from his superior height, taking my hand down away from my throat and pulling it down between us. He held it loosely but firmly, and I knew I wasn't going anywhere anytime soon.

He wasn't hurting me at all, but he was seriously scaring me. He was just standing there holding my hand, looking down at me in the dark. That was when I caught a whiff of the alcohol on his breath. Crap!

"Um... nothing. Nothing is the matter," I answered as calmly as I could while I tried to pull my hand away from him. His hold tightened perceptibly. He definitely wasn't ready to let go.

"You know something, Chunky?" Chad asked in a conversational-like tone.

Humor him, I told myself. Humor him until Peanut gets out here then we could both escape back into the house together. "No Chad. What?" I returned in a tone that I hoped matched his. I was also trying very hard not to notice how he was slurring his words.

"I've been watching you," he drawled out, making me stiffen. I already knew he had been, which was creepy, but hearing him admit it out loud was far creepier. "And do you know what I've noticed?" he continued on, the hand clasping mine starting to swing back and forth in a surprisingly gentle and nonthreatening motion.

"Umm... no," I answered, trying once again to pull my hand away from his. As gentle and nonthreatening as his hold was, he was still holding me against my will. He was really starting to freak me out a bit. "What did you notice?" I asked with another subtle tug of my arm.

Chad laughed like I'd said something funny. *Or* he laughed because I kept trying to get my hand free from him. Either way, his laugh chilled me.

"I noticed that you always watch Scott," Chad suddenly stated with startling force. "You stare at him and you watch him and I can tell you want him," Chad rambled in an angry tone. "I can tell you like him. Does he make you hot, Chunky?" Chad continued and his tone and voice got rougher and louder as he put his face right down into mine. I started pulling at my hands in earnest then, but he wouldn't let me go. I was about to start screaming for help when suddenly and without any warning, Chad lowered his forehead and rested it on mine, whispering, "Maybe he gets you so hot you need a minute to cool off."

And before I knew it, Chad twisted his entire upper body to the right, before swinging it *and* me back around to the left. I was airborne for mere seconds before gravity finally took effect and I dropped like a stone. In seconds I was submerged in a world of water. I was in the deep end of Dean Scott's swimming pool.

10. Dazed and Confused

For the briefest moment I thought I was going to drown. In the madness of the last few moments, I had completely forgotten that I knew how to swim. Thankfully, the survival instinct kicked in and I fought my way back up to the top. I gulped in deep breaths of air as my head broke the water's surface. The first thing I noticed was that I felt weighted down and I knew it was because of my clothes. Wet shirt, pants, and shoes, no matter how light weight, made swimming a little more difficult than usual.

The second thing I noticed was loud voices and even a few screams. With my heart racing and shallow gasps of air escaping from between my lips, I silently treaded water to allot my brain much needed time to assimilate everything. Then I remembered Chad and I figured time, quite possibly, wasn't on my side. A quick glance around reassured me. I didn't know where he had gone, but he wasn't standing there anymore and that's all I really currently cared about.

"Chunky!" a female voice yelled. "What in the world are you doing?" Peanut screeched as she ran toward me. It was hard not to notice Dean, David, Butter and a host of other people running my way. I groaned. Maybe it would have been better if I'd drowned.

"What does it look like?" I asked in an offhand manner. A part of me knew that I was in some kind of shock. Between Chad scaring the wits out of me, and his bright idea to "cool me off" I felt far from okay. But for some strange reason, I also felt like laughing and that just made me want to cry.

"Someone pushed her into the pool," Sara Jones said from somewhere to the right of me.

"Who?" Dean, David and Butter simultaneously roared.

I had to admit that that made me feel kind of better. I liked the thought of my men getting all manly on my behalf. A girl could get used to it. I giggled. They all looked at me as if I'd lost my head. That made me giggle again, which made me swallow water, which made me start choking. I had the feeling that was when Dean decided enough was enough. Because I watched in shock as he toed off his Dockers, stripped off his shirt, and dove into the pool. In seconds, he had his arm around my neck and was tugging me toward the side of the pool. Once there, Butter and David pulled me up while Dean pushed.

"Hey!" I yelled suddenly. "Hands!" His hands had been on my...

"Sorry," Dean muttered.

I giggled again but this time the giggles turned into tears and I started crying in earnest. While I sobbed my teeth chattered until I thought I'd chip a tooth.

"Here," a voice said from above my head. I felt a large warm towel being wrapped around me. Whoever wrapped the towel around me, had wrapped themselves around me as well, and held and rocked me while I cried.

"Who pushed her into the pool?" Dean asked from right by my ear. It was then that I realized Dean was the one holding me.

"I don't know," Sara answered. "I could really only see two shadows close together. I thought it was a couple making out so I really didn't pay attention. I didn't even know it was Chunky until after she was in the water."

I felt Dean stiffen but I didn't pay it much attention. I was too busy enjoying the warmth and security of his arms holding me. I was only just starting to feel the trembling lighten up.

"Kissing?" Peanut demanded. "Chunky wouldn't have been kissing anyone," she declared absolutely. Of course, Peanut and I both knew that wasn't really true because I quite probably would have kissed Dean—under different circumstances of course.

"Hey guys. She's okay, but let's give her some space. Thanks," Dean said as David and Butter ushered people away from where I sat like a drowned rat and back to the party.

"Hey, are you okay?" Dean asked.

"Hmm," I murmured, starting to feel a little sleepy which was really weird since I was drenched from head to toe.

"What happened?" Peanut asked after an awkward second. "Open your eyes Chunky and tell us what happened!" she demanded one last time in that tone of voice I knew meant she would never go away and leave me alone if I didn't give in and do what she said.

I opened my eyes. Water dripped down into them and I had to close them again. Taking an edge of the towel, I swiped at the offending rivulets as they ran down my cheeks.

"Come here," Dean urged as he withdrew his arms from around me then stood up, only to walk around to the front of me, grab my hands and pull me up to my feet. "Let's get you somewhere a little more comfortable, shall we."

"Good idea," Peanut approved. She was fussing around me like a mother hen. I smiled at her to let her know that I was okay, dreading the explanation, but okay.

I glanced around as Dean led me over to a cream-colored cushioned pool lounger. I figured Chad was probably long gone by now, but I couldn't be too careful. While I looked around for Chad, I was thankful to see that Butter and David had ushered everyone else away to give us some privacy. So no Chad and no crowd meant my luck was improving.

Wrapping the towel tightly around my shoulders, I slid down into the comfortable chair.

"I wasn't kissing anybody!" I suddenly shouted.

Peanut and Dean looked at each other in concern, before turning back to me. "Okay," Dean and Peanut said simultaneously, obviously trying to appease me.

I groaned. I didn't appear to be making much sense to them. "I heard what Sara said," I tried to clarify. "That she thought whoever was standing over here was making out. Well, I wasn't," I said. "We *weren't*," I adamantly declared.

"Who's we, Chunky?" Peanut quietly asked.

"Chad," I answered in a whisper. I could hardly bring myself to speak his name out loud. He had truly scared me tonight in a way I knew would stick with me for some time to come.

Peanut sat down on the edge of the lounger and put her arm around me, while Dean crouched down in front of me and rested his hand over both of mine. It was then that I noticed my left hand rubbing at the right one; the one that Chad had grabbed and wouldn't let go of.

"Tell us what happened, Chunky," Peanut ordered. "You'll probably feel better if you do."

A dry laugh left my throat but held no real humor. "I doubt it," I said.

"Try anyway," Dean encouraged.

I wanted to rub my head to try to clear it but Dean's hand was over both of mine and I didn't want to lose that contact, so I resisted the urge. Instead, I thought back over those frightening and strange moments with Chad. I frowned trying to understand the entire point of the encounter. Why had he been so mean? Why was he so angry with me?

"I really can only tell you what happened," I finally tried to explain. "But I have absolutely no explanation for the why of it. I came outside like I told you I was, Peanut. It's gorgeous out here, by the way," I added casually in an aside to Dean.

He murmured, "Thank you," but didn't say another word.

85

He obviously recognized a stalling technique when he heard one. So I started talking again.

"There were a few groups of people talking so I tried to stay away from them and I walked toward the other side near where you found me. It was secluded and I liked that."

Peanut nodded her head at me. Peanut knew very well my tendency toward private-like settings. She could see quite easily how I would end up where I did. I smiled at her for understanding me so well.

"I was standing there when I realized how much time had passed so I decided to turn around and head back toward the house to look for Peanut." I turned to look at Peanut for my own explanation of where she had been. I didn't even have to voice the question.

"I ran into Butter and Veronica. I stayed for a few minutes to talk. I was getting ready to come out and find you when Sara screamed for help. I got out here in time to see you take your first gulp of air," she admitted with a grimace of her lips.

"Oh, okay," I said. "That makes sense."

When I didn't say anything else, Dean squeezed my hand. I instinctively tried to jerk my hand away from him and stand up at the same time. I just wanted to get away.

"What the hell?" Dean growled, while Peanut tried to calm me down. "What in the world did he do to her?"

Suddenly I stopped trying to escape and a quiet sob escaped. "I'm sorry," I whispered collapsing back down onto the lounger.

Peanut and Dean murmured soothing words but for the life of me I couldn't register what they were saying. This was so silly, I thought to myself. Yeah, Chad had scared me to death but it wasn't like he had been beating me or trying to rape me. Why was I reacting so spastically?

"Sorry," I whispered again, before clearing my throat. Dean crouched back down in front of me, but this time he didn't touch me. I hated that. I didn't want him to think I didn't like his touch, but I didn't have the nerve to reach out and touch him to let him know it was okay.

"Finish," Dean ordered and I noticed for the first time that he looked very tense and angry. No dimples made an appearance. In fact, his jaw kept flexing and I could tell he was gritting his teeth. I hoped he wasn't angry at me.

"I was turning around to head back inside," I repeated, "when suddenly a shadow appeared in front of me. It was Chad. He grabbed my hand," I said, grabbing my own hand, the one he had grabbed. I started rubbing it again. Dean's eyes watched and flared when he noted my gesture. Understanding lightened his expression.

"That's why you acted like that when I squeezed your hand," he deducted.

I shrugged at him. "I guess."

"Go on," Peanut prompted me when I stayed quiet for longer than she liked.

"It was Chad and he was holding my hand and getting up in my face saying stupid things."

"What things?" Dean asked.

I was not about to go there. There was no way I'd tell him what Chad said. They were stupid things and had no real bearing to the story.

"Just *things*!" I repeated making it clear by my tone that I didn't have any plan on elaborating further than that. "He was just being a creep. I could smell alcohol on his breath. At first, I thought it would be best if I just tried to humor him. I knew Peanut was coming out, and I just had to stall him for a few minutes."

"Oh Chunky, I'm so sorry," Peanut groaned.

"Not your fault," I assured her. "It was Chad's. He grabbed my hand, talked some smack and threw me into the pool for kicks. That's all. I don't even know why I'm reacting so badly to this." I finished with a groan. I could feel the tears pressing against the back of my eyes but I didn't want them to fall.

"You're upset because Chad basically assaulted you Chunky!" Peanut insisted. "He held you against your will, verbally abused you, and then proceeded to physically move you. If that doesn't say assault to you then you need to start reading some of your daddy's detective books."

Dean groaned. "Your dad's a detective?"

"Yeah," I answered defensively. I was a little disappointed in Dean at his reaction to the news that my dad was a detective. It was obvious he would have rather kept this quiet than take the chance on getting into some sort of trouble.

"This sucks!" he said, straightening up and running his hands through his hair.

I stood up to. His reaction on top of everything else was too much. "Well, I'm so sorry that you're so inconvenienced. I'll just leave and…"

"Hey…" Dean said in a soothing voice. "I…"

"I know what you meant. You're afraid you'll get into trouble if my dad, the detective, gets called to your house. Well, don't worry, Butter can…"

"Stop it!" Dean barked and I shut up. "I was not upset about that," he said in aggravation.

"Then what were you upset about?" I asked skeptically.

Dean put his hand on his cocked hip and looked at me in disbelief. "How would you like to be in my position?" he half-growled. When I continued to stare at him in confusion he threw his head back and groaned.

"Come on," he said, sweeping his arm out around him to indicate our surroundings. "I'm new here. I've thrown a party that my friend, *you*, came to and you got accosted by a very stupid, very drunk boy. An *underage* drunk boy," he clarified. "And instead of getting to meet my new friend's dad in the more usual manner, I have to meet him over the telephone to explain to him that I need him to come to my home because his daughter was abused while under my protection. And to find out your dad is not just any dad, but a police detective of all things... Can you possibly understand how most guys in my position would hate, absolutely dread the upcoming meeting, or should I say confrontation? It's not exactly the kind of first impression a guy dreams of, you know!"

I hung my head. "I'm sorry," I whispered.

Dean released a loud gush of air and immediately walked over to me and wrapped me up into his arms. "Please don't *you* apologize to *me*. I should be apologizing to you. It's not bad enough that Chad pulled this stunt, but that I feel somehow justified in yelling at you because I don't think you're being sympathetic enough to my feelings, is ridiculous."

"We don't have to call my dad," I offered but I could feel Dean shake his head no.

"We're definitely calling your dad," he stated emphatically, "if for no other reason than this needs to be reported. Chad can't get away with what he's done. If we let him, he just might try it again."

That thought chilled me and I groaned my denial into Dean's neck. A neck and chest I was starting to realize was still bare. The warmth of his skin, despite having been wet only a short time before, was seeping through my wet shirt and I wanted to stay there for the rest of the night. I didn't want to let go; I didn't want to think about what had happened; and I most definitely did not want to have to call my dad.

Heavy footsteps sounded close by. "Your dad is on his way, Chunky," Butter announced into the silence and I groaned again, this time only longer and louder.

11. The After Party

"I've sent everyone home," David spoke into the deafening silence.

I released Dean abruptly and took a step back. Though the comfort of his arms called to me, I resisted. After everything else, the last thing my dad needed was to walk in here and see me draped all over some half-dressed guy he didn't know. It didn't matter how harmless or innocent the hug was, I didn't want my dad's first time seeing me in the arms of a boy to be tonight. As it was, I didn't really know what to expect or how my dad was going to react once he got here.

I saw Dean grimace. "What?" I asked.

"I'm not too sure sending everyone home was a good idea, is all."

"Why not?" David asked with a frown. "I figured her dad wouldn't freak out as bad if he just saw us and not a huge crowd. Plus I thought Chunky would prefer it."

Dean gave a dry chuckle without much humor. "But did you know her dad was a *police detective*?" he asked, stressing the two last words.

"Umm...no. No I didn't know that," David replied looking ill at ease at the news. "Man, Mom and Dad are going to be ticked."

Dean chuckled with humor at that. "I'm a little more worried about her dad right now."

"What happened, anyway?" Butter spoke up. "Sara said she saw Chunky kissing some guy then the next thing she knew Chunky was landing with a loud splash in the pool."

"I was not kissing him!" I yelled at Butter. I absolutely, positively did not want anyone to think that I had been kissing Chad Williams.

"Hey, hey. It's okay," Dean soothed, closing the distance between us and raising his hand to my damp, tangled hair, pushing it out of my eyes. "Butter didn't mean anything by that. He was only repeating what Sara said she *assumed* was happening out here. We'll make sure everything is cleared up."

Frustrated and worried and so overwhelmed by the entire evening, I couldn't withhold the lone tear that escaped from my eye to trek down my cheek. Dean reached out and wiped it away with his thumb before it could reach my mouth.

He gave me one of his sweet smiles. "I think we've gotten wet enough tonight, don't you?" he murmured in a teasing tone.

I sniffed back anymore tears before they could escape, returned his smile with a weak one of my own, and nodded my head in agreement.

"So what did happen?" Butter asked again.

"That's what I'd like to know," my dad's voice boomed from several feet away. "And I want to know right now!" he finished as his long strides ate up the short distance to where we all stood.

"Chunky!" he said, grabbing me into a bear hug, before stepping back and holding me at arm's length to give me a thorough once over. "Any particular reason you decided to swim in your clothes?" he gruffly asked.

I could tell my dad was trying to regain control. Now that he had seen me and knew that I was fine his parental fear was fading away and the cop in him wanted answers. Only this time, the victim was me and he was finding it a little harder to step into his habitual role of detective. His attempt at humor was more for himself than me.

I leaned up on tiptoe and whispered solemnly, "I forgot to shave my legs. That's why I decided to swim in my clothes."

Dad chuckled, a more natural sound, and gave me one last hug before stepping back and looking around at everyone standing there.

"Is this everyone that was here tonight?" he asked with skepticism.

I could hear Dean and David groan simultaneously from behind me. I started to answer but Dean stepped forward before I could say a word.

"No sir."

My dad looked at Dean for a long moment. "And you are?" he coldly asked.

I saw Dean swallow noticeably. "I'm Dean. Dean Scott, sir." Dean answered when suddenly David stepped forward as well.

"And I'm David Scott, sir. This is our home and our party," he answered forthrightly.

My dad gave a slight nod. "So where is everyone?" he asked, looking around.

"That's my fault," David immediately answered. "I was trying to make things easier on Chunky and," he hesitated and looked a little embarrassed. "And well... you. I didn't stop to think that you might want to talk with them. I didn't know..." David instantly cut off.

"Didn't know what?" my dad prompted.

"We didn't know that you were a police detective, sir," Dean stepped into the conversation. "We didn't consider that you might want to make this more... official?"

"What exactly is *this*?" my dad asked with his hands held

open. "All I know is what Butter said into the telephone and that was pretty cryptic."

Dad turned to look at Butter. "'Royal, Chunky was pushed into the pool and she's crying. You better come,' is what you said to me Butter. I thought she'd hurt herself." Dad turned back to look at me. "And considering the way Chunky looks I think she was hurt but just not in the way I imagined."

Dad looked up at Dean and David then back down at me. "So who wants to tell me what really happened—and I mean all of it, so I can decide whether we need to make this *official* or not?"

Dean started to speak up but I cut him off. "I'll tell him," I said to Dean, before turning back to my dad.

"It's not their fault," I told my dad, looking over at Dean and David. "They had nothing to do with any of it."

"I think you need to let me be the judge of that, Chunky," my dad cut in, before I could defend Dean or David again. "I just want you to tell me what happened and I'll decide who's at fault."

In the mood my dad was in, I knew to listen to him. I knew Dean and David hadn't done anything and that truth would come out in the course of my story. So, gathering all of my remaining strength, I recited what had happened to me to my dad as clearly and efficiently as I could.

"I came out here because I wanted to see the pool and backyard," I started saying but my dad quickly jumped in.

"By yourself?" he demanded.

"No!" Peanut jumped in, in my defense. "Well, yes," she quickly amended. "But..."

Dad held his hand up for Peanut to stop talking. She did.

"Dad!" I half-groaned. "Let me finish telling you everything before you ask questions."

"Okay, you're right. Go on." He nodded at me to proceed.

I nodded back. "Anyway, Peanut needed to use the bathroom. It was getting kind of stuffy inside so I told her

I was going to go on outside and she should meet me there. Nobody was swimming but a few people were sitting on the pool's edge and talking. I walked over to there," I said, pointing to where I was referring to. "After a few minutes, when Peanut hadn't come out, I decided to go looking for her. But before I could, this shadow appeared and I jumped further back. The shadow became a boy..."

I tried to keep explaining, but my hands started trembling when I remembered how scared I had started to feel when Chad grabbed my hand and had pushed his face into mine.

A large hand suddenly reached out and gripped one of my trembling ones. Fingers intertwined with fingers. Startled, I looked down. I wasn't surprised to find Dean's hand engulfing mine. I quickly looked up to my dad, but he wasn't looking at me. His eyes were trained on my hand and the other hand that was holding it so tightly. I saw his jaw twitch but he didn't say a word.

"Who was the boy?" he finally asked a bit gruffly.

"Chad Williams," Dean spoke up and answered. I had a feeling Dean knew I didn't want to say Chad's name aloud.

"Chad?" my dad asked with surprise.

I nodded my head up and down. "He's been," I paused, looking for the right words to describe how Chad had been acting lately.

"He's been acting like a real weirdo," Peanut chimed in, ever helpful. "All week since school started back, he's been staring at Chunky and acting all creepy like. And today, this morning, he said some unforgivable things about Chunky in front of a lot of people and..."

"Peanut!" I interjected before she could say anything else.

"Well, your dad needs to know Chunky and if you're not going to tell him then I am!" Peanut responded unrepentantly.

I glanced up at my dad and he was glaring back down at me. "You came to this party knowing he was going to be here?"

"No!" I answered immediately. "I didn't think Ch... he

would be here at all. He doesn't seem to like Dean because of the whole football thing. I never thought he'd show up here tonight."

"Why didn't you tell me about any of this other stuff?" my dad demanded to know.

"Because I thought he was just being a jerk!"

"Tell me the rest!" my dad ordered after a very tense pause.

I had to take a minute to remember where I had left off. Clearing my throat and squeezing Dean's hand that thankfully still retained possession of mine, I finished telling the story.

"Ch...Chad grabbed my hand, not real hard, just tight enough so I couldn't get away. He said a few things. I could smell alcohol on his breath because at one time he pressed his face close to mine. That was when I really started to get worried. So I decided to placate him, you know. I thought, if I can just go along with him until Peanut comes out and sees and then she'll get help and everything would be fine," I paused to take a breath.

"But it wasn't," my dad stated.

I looked at him sadly. "No, not really. He made a few more comments, and before I knew it, he was twisting his body one way then twisting it back and throwing me into the water. The next thing I know, I'm flying through the air before being swallowed up by thousands of gallons of water." I raked my free hand through my still damp hair. "It happened so fast and I hadn't been expecting it in the least," I looked at my dad imploringly. "I couldn't stop him."

"How could you even think you could, Chunky," Butter demanded. "He probably weighs about eighty more pounds than you and he's solid muscle," Butter slapped his hand on his thigh in anger and disgust. "He shouldn't have had his hands on you at all!" he growled.

"Son," Dad cautioned Butter. "You need to stay calm. Chad will be taken care of, but in the right way," he warned.

Butter hung his head then nodded it in agreement. "Yes sir," he mumbled.

"Good," my dad approved, before looking up and making eye contact with everyone present, which included Dean, David, Peanut, Eric, Butter and myself. "That goes for all of you. No payback. No eye for an eye. I don't even want you guys talking about this at school or with your other friends," Dad warned.

"I'm sorry, sir," Dean interjected and all eyes turned toward him. "But I don't know if I can agree to that."

My jaw dropped. Peanut's, Butter's, Eric's, and David's jaws dropped. We all stared at him as if he had lost his mind. I waited with bated breath for my dad's reaction. I was pretty impressed with his calm demeanor but I didn't trust it for a minute.

"And why wouldn't you be able to agree to that?" my dad asked Dean in a conversational tone, just as if he was asking him if he would like fries with that.

Dean cleared his throat. It was obvious he was very nervous. "Because Sara, a girl that was here tonight intimated that whoever was over in the dark with her was... well..." Dean coughed again.

"Was what, son?" my dad asked with suspicion.

"Making out. Kissing," he rushed out. "But they weren't. She wasn't. But it was dark and Sara said she assumed that that was what was going on. She said she hadn't even known it was her until after Ch...your daughter was in the water. So *we* know she wasn't getting close up and personal with Chad, but by tomorrow, after the story gets spread around, everyone else isn't going to be so sure."

"Oh God!" I groaned, dropping my head into my hand. "That hadn't even occurred to me."

Dean squeezed my hand in silent support and sympathy.

My dad crossed his hands over his chest and rocked back and forth on his feet for a few seconds. It was obvious he

96

was contemplating what Dean had said and weighing the ramifications. I worried what that meant for me.

"Well, I'm going to call this in and have a patrolman ride out here so we can file a report. Chad's actions were a step too close to something more serious, and this needs to be documented. He also needs to know that behavior like that will not be condoned. His parents will be notified as well." Dad gave a tired sigh and reached up to rub at his baldhead. "Did anyone else see Chad here tonight?"

Everyone shook their heads no. Dad grimaced.

"Do you know if any one here tonight at the party saw Chad? Anyone who will admit it," Dad quickly clarified.

"We'd have to ask around," David said, before adding, "I guess it really wasn't a good idea to send everyone home."

Dad cocked his eye at him but didn't say anything in response. "It will mainly cause problems for Chunky."

"What do you mean?" I asked.

"We can still file the report. And we are. But as far as stopping any rumors go it'll mainly be a he said she said thing. And in my experience, people are going to believe what they want."

"Meaning?" Butter asked.

"Meaning," Dad answered with a sigh. "That no matter how hard anyone of you try to deny that Chunky wasn't kissing Chad but instead being harassed by him, in the end it won't matter because there will always be those people who want to believe the worst. I mean you could try. But if you try too hard, you run the risk of it looking even more suspicious."

"But that's not fair!" Peanut snapped. "Chunky can't stand Chad. There's no way she'd give him the time of day!"

"No one said it was fair, Peanut," my dad said with a sad smile. "Just that, that was the way it was. I think, for Chunky's sake, the less said, the better, especially where Chad is concerned. He will be visited and warned, you can believe that, but he'll be back at school with you all on Monday, and Chunky is the one who will have to face him and everybody else. It should ultimately be up to her how she wants this handled."

"That's true," Dean quickly agreed. "But it seems there should be some way we could make it clear that she was the victim."

I grimaced at that word. "I don't want to be anyone's victim," I said softly. "Even if it means I have to wade through some stupid gossip, I won't be *Chad's* victim. And if things get too bad," I said in a louder voice, feeling more hopeful than I had since this whole debacle had started, "I'll just have to make a hundred copies of the police report and stick them on the windows of every car in the school parking lot."

Peanut giggled. "And I'll help!"

Everyone else laughed and cheered and said they would help as well.

I looked up at my dad. "I think you're right. There's a part of me that wishes you weren't so I could rush home and call everyone that I know who was here and tell them exactly what happened. But people *are* going to believe what they want and there were a bunch of people who were here tonight who would prefer the juicer version to the true one."

Suddenly the sound of two sets of footsteps could be heard walking our way. Dean and David groaned at the same time. Everyone turned at once and looked up at the two nicely dressed people that stood on the back porch looking down at them in confusion.

"Nice party?" the man who was obviously Dean and David's father asked with evident sarcasm and a smidgen of anger.

12. Meeting the Parents

"Hi Mom," Dean said.

"Hi Dad," David said.

"Dean. David," their dad acknowledged them with a nod. "What's going on here?" he asked in a way that I thought was a bit too casual.

My dad looked to Dean and David, before turning back to their parents and walking over to them. The rest of us followed along silently. Dean and David's parents met my dad halfway. By the time we reached them the introductions had been made and Dean's dad could be heard saying, "And you're a police detective?"

"Yes sir," my dad was answering, before turning toward me and pointing. "And the one there that looks like a drowned rat is my daughter, Chunky."

"Chunky?" Dean and David's mother asked with curiosity.

"It's a nickname," Dean quickly spoke up.

"Oh," Dean's mother replied. "I see."

By the expression on her face, I didn't really think she did, but by the expression on their dad's face, I didn't really think he thought it was important at all.

"So what's going on Dean? David?" their father asked,

looking at first at one son and then the other. "You both swore to your Mother and me that this would be a harmless get together. We discussed this and we agreed that at the slightest hint of a problem, you would call us at the club a few blocks away, so that we could come home immediately. Well, it appears that the party wasn't so harmless and we've come home to find a police detective, no less, in our home. So will one of you kindly explain to me why you shouldn't be grounded for the next three months?"

I quickly glanced over at Dean. He was standing there silently hanging his head in shame, not even trying to defend himself. It wasn't fair! This whole night wasn't fair. I turned to my dad looking for help. He had already started talking before my eyes even landed on him.

"Sir, Ma'am," my dad was saying in his most professional voice.

"Please call us Derrick and Moira," Dean's dad offered.

"Thank you," my dad responded. "And call me Royal," my dad reciprocated. "Derrick, Moira, evidently a young man that has already been named, crashed the party tonight unbeknownst to either of your sons. This boy, Chad..."

"Chad Williams?" Derrick Scott broke in to ask. "The other quarterback for the Wolverines?"

"The one and the same," my dad confirmed. "He showed up, or I guess you could say he snuck in, as none of the kids here were even aware that he was in attendance at the party. He had alcohol on his breath. He harassed and grabbed my daughter as well as threw her into the swimming pool fully clothed. At which time," Dad paused and turned toward Dean. "I believe Dean jumped in to help her. All of this, you understand, happened with no witness to collaborate it except for Chunky, who, I assure you, I believe. Not only because she is my daughter but also because of what the other kids here have revealed about Chad's behavior at school."

Moira and Derrick Scott nodded their head in unison.

"Royal, we've also had some issues with the Williams boy and his father, over football. Chad's behavior at times has been quite startling and his father's as well," Moira Scott confided.

I looked over to Butter then David and then Dean to watch their expressions. None of them had said one word about any of this. I knew there was probably some serious rivalry going on between Chad and Dean, but to hear the Scott's talk, it appeared that there was a little more to it than that.

I was shocked even more when my dad nodded his head in response and said, "I am very familiar with Chris Williams." What did he mean by that?

"Are you all right?" Derrick Scott asked me.

I nodded my head. "Yes sir. I was just scared at first."

"Of course you were, dear," Moira Scott clucked. "And I'm sure you're very uncomfortable standing there in those damp clothes."

I smiled slightly at her. "Now that you mention it..."

My dad instantly turned and looked at me. "Why didn't you say so?"

Moira Scott looked at me and laughed softly. "I would imagine Royal that your daughter thought you had more important things on your mind right now than whether she was uncomfortable."

My dad glanced down at his watch. "I need to call the precinct and get a car out here to take everyone's statement. It will be at least another hour before anyone can leave," he said looking down at me and my sodden clothes. "I wish I'd thought to bring you a change of clothes, but I left in a rush and didn't give it a thought," he groused, rubbing at his baldhead again.

"Of course you didn't, Royal," Mrs. Scott soothed. "Your instinct was to get to your child. I'm sure I can wrestle something up for her to change into so she can be more comfortable."

"I'm fine," I said when I actually felt like screaming, "Heck no." Mrs. Scott was almost as tiny as Peanut and though Mr. Scott was taller than both of his sons, he was lean. There was no way that this family had anything in their home that was going to fit me. And I didn't want to be standing around everyone an hour from now when that fact became obvious.

"Don't be silly," my dumb dad said. "Go with Mrs. Scott and find something warm and dry to change into."

"I'll come with you," Peanut offered helpfully, skipping over to where Mrs. Scott stood. Both of them looked at me expectantly. Accepting that I didn't really have any other option, I slowly shuffled over to join them.

"Good," Mrs. Scott said. "That's settled. We're going to step inside now. You boys fill your father in on everything that happened tonight," she ordered, before ushering Peanut and I toward the back screen door. As we stepped up onto the back porch, Mrs. Scott suddenly stopped and turned back to the others. "Dean," she called. "You need to get inside and put on a shirt and dry pants!"

She waited for Dean's, "Yes Ma'am," before walking towards the back door once again. Just as Peanut and I were about to cross the threshold, Mrs. Scott suddenly stopped a second time and turned back to hers sons. "Oh and boys," she caroled. "It probably goes without saying, but I'll say it nonetheless. There will be no more un-chaperoned parties." Mrs. Scott didn't wait for a response this time but continued walking into her house.

Peanut and I silently followed after her. We followed her up a flight of stairs and into a bedroom. "This is our guestroom," Mrs. Scott explained. "Mary, my sister used it recently. She's always leaving things behind when she visits. Let me check the closet," she said, opening the large closet doors and stepping inside. "Here we go," we heard her call from deep inside. Mrs. Scott stepped back out clutching a fluffy purple bathrobe. "Perfect," she declared, holding it up toward me. "The bathroom is in through there," she told me pointing toward a closed door. "Change into the robe then we'll go downstairs to the utility room and put your clothes into the dryer. They won't be in the best shape but at least they'll be dry."

I walked into the bathroom and quickly shut the door. I had every intention of changing out of my clothes as fast as I could, but when I turned on the bathroom light I couldn't believe my eyes. The bathroom was amazing! There was a shower that would easily fit four people with three shower heads sitting strategically in the stall. The way it was designed, water would spray out from every angle as a person showered. There was also a large Jacuzzi-style tub and a double-sink vanity. It was all done in a beautiful hunter green tile with intricate designs.

I stood in the center of the bathroom feeling dumbstruck. And this was just the guest bathroom, I thought to myself. Shaking my head, I unbuttoned my khakis and started to undress. Peeling damp pants off of damp skin was a lot harder and more tedious than I ever thought it could be.

Whisking off the rest of my clothes I quickly scrambled into the plush purple robe that Mrs. Scott had provided me. I gathered my discarded clothes up into my arms and reached for the light switch to turn the lights off. That was when I noticed the bathroom came equipped with heated room and heated floors. "Amazing," I whispered as I turned out the lights and stepped back out into the guest bedroom.

Peanut was sitting on the edge of the bed waiting for me. "Mrs. Scott told us to make our way downstairs when you were done," Peanut informed me.

"How bad do I look?" I asked Peanut, holding my wet clothes in one arm while extending the other so Peanut could get a good look.

"Like a fluffy purple bunny?" Peanut teased.

I frowned back at her. "Seriously?"

"You look fine," she assured me. "But forget how you look. How do you feel? I can't believe Chad treated you like that. What's gotten into him? I mean don't get me wrong, he's *never* been a prince, but I can't remember him being *bad*."

"I don't know," I shuddered, remembering his awful behavior. "What do you think my dad meant when he said he was familiar with Chad's dad? And remember what the Scott's said about Chad and his dad?"

"Yeah, I heard but I haven't got a clue. I'm gonna ask Butter later and see if he knows anything."

"I have a feeling everyone on the team knows something, but I don't think they'll talk. Not even Butter," I added when Peanut started to speak.

"Come on," Peanut said as she jumped up off of the bed. "We need to get downstairs. That policeman is coming and he might already be here to get our statement."

I didn't move. I was very conscious of being naked under the robe—a very unbecoming fluffy purple robe. This was just too awkward.

Peanut was already out the door when she realized that I wasn't following behind her. She turned around to look at me over her shoulder. "You look fine, Chunky. Plus it's too late and everyone is too tired to notice what you look like. Besides, "she added with a grin. "I noticed Dean holding your hand when you looked like, how was it your dad described you, a drowned rat? Well, this is definitely an improvement. So I'd say you have nothing to worry about."

I threw my wet shirt at her. Peanut ducked away from the wet missile and laughed back at me as she dashed off down the stairs, calling back, "Missed!"

Rolling my eyes at her retreating back, I bent over to pick up the wet shirt. A pair of feet suddenly appeared; a very large pair of lightly tanned feet. I grabbed my shirt and slowly stood back up.

"Hi," Dean said, staring down at me.

"Hi," I answered back.

Dean kind of did a little shuffle before saying, "I wanted to check that you were okay."

I nodded. "I'm fine. A bit embarrassed, but fine."

Dean frowned. "Why do you feel embarrassed?"

I swept my hand out. "Because all this drama. It's all because of me. You're in trouble with your parents. I'm pretty sure I'm in trouble with my dad. Chad is definitely going to be in trouble. I mean come on, Dean a police officer is coming to your house to take our statements—because of me and that is so embarrassing!"

"First of all, my parents aren't that mad at David and me because we didn't do anything wrong. They're mostly mad at themselves for giving into our request to go ahead with the party even though they knew they wouldn't be here. Second, I'd say your dad is just glad you're okay and if I had to guess, I'd say he's mostly angry with himself for letting you come to a party that wasn't going to be chaperoned. As for Chad, I sure hope he gets into trouble after what he's done. If I hadn't already agreed to let things go, I'd probably be out with David, Eric, and Butter right now hunting him down. As for the policeman coming to my house, he's already here and he seems like a very nice guy. So as far as I can see, you have absolutely nothing to be embarrassed about."

I looked down at my bare toes peeking at me from under the robe. An inner glow was growing inside me as I replayed everything Dean had just said. Dean was such a champion. A golden boy. As cheesy as it sounded, he was a good guy. I smiled. He just always made me want to smile.

"What about this robe? Should I be embarrassed to wear this?" I asked, while still smiling.

Dean's dimples appeared. "Absolutely not. You look like a precious purple bunny rabbit."

"Peanut!" I growled in mock anger causing Dean to laugh out loud.

"She told me to tell you that's what you looked like when she passed me on the stairs," he confided still laughing.

"Some best friend," I muttered to myself as I followed Dean down the stairs.

105

My good humor lasted until we reached the kitchen. My dad was there along with everyone else. Peanut was finishing up her short statement.

"Butter," my dad said. "You can go ahead and take Eric and Peanut home."

"Yes sir," Butter murmured.

"Oh and Butter, Peanut," my dad said, halting their exit. "I'll assume that by the time I talk with your parents tomorrow they'll already know about everything that has transpired here tonight."

"Yes sir!" they answered.

"I'll call you tomorrow, Chunky," Peanut said.

But before I could say anything my dad started talking. "Actually Peanut, I think it would be best that you don't call." At Peanut's shocked expression my dad held his hand up in a placating manner. "I'm not mad at you and I don't blame you for anything. I think tonight's been enough for everyone and Chunky needs a quiet weekend."

"I agree," Moira Scott interjected. "Dean and David won't be doing anything this weekend but cleaning up this mess. I think a quiet weekend is what all of you need."

Peanut frowned but didn't say anything. My dad smiled at her. "Peanut, I'm sure by the time I'm finished talking with your dad tomorrow, he'll agree too."

Mr. and Mrs. Scott laughed along with the police officer. The rest of us obviously didn't see the humor. When that became apparent, the adults laughed even harder.

Goodbyes were then quickly exchanged and Peanut, Butter and Eric left.

"Boys," Derrick Scott said. "Let's give Chunky and her dad some privacy," indicating with his hand that they should leave the room.

"Bye Chunky," David said as he walked out of the room. "Hope you feel better."

Dean looked over at me like he wanted to say something,

but before he spoke he gave a quick glance over at my dad. Whatever he saw had him changing his mind. "Goodnight," he finally said instead. "Remember what I told you," he reminded me, before turning away and walking out of the kitchen followed by his parents.

"Okay, Chunky," my dad said. "Let's get this over with and this time," he paused significantly, "I want to know exactly what those *things* were, that Chad had said."

The next twenty minutes were gruesome. Having to repeat what Chad said to me in front of my dad was probably one of the worst experiences of my life. He sat quietly through it all. His face didn't change expressions once, but the slight tick in his jaw spoke volumes. Finally and thankfully I was done. The police officer said he would get it typed up and I would need to come by the precinct to sign the official statement. Dad told him he would bring me down tomorrow.

Great, I thought to myself, at least I had something to look forward to this weekend. Apparently I was going to be on lock down for what was left of the rest of the weekend. I wondered if I would get only bread and water to eat. At my last thought, I realized I was getting a little giddy. And tired. I was really, really tired. I slumped into the chair I was sitting in.

"Chunky," Mrs. Scott said suddenly appearing in front of me. "Here are your clothes. Don't bother changing now. Just return the robe when you get a chance," she said smiling at me.

"Thank you," I mumbled sleepily.

"You're welcome," she murmured back. She grinned at my father. "I think she's exhausted," she told him.

My dad nodded his head. "She's always gotten like this when she gets overtired. She'll probably talk in her sleep tonight, too."

Mrs. Scott smiled at my dad. "My David is like that too, but don't tell him I told you so."

Dad winked at her. "No Ma'am. I won't say a word."

Dad put his arm around me and pulled me up out of the chair. "Let's go, Chunky," he said having to half-carry me to the door. He stopped and turned back to the Scott's. "It was a pleasure meeting both of you. Hopefully next time it will be under better circumstances."

The Scott's quickly agreed and good nights were exchanged before Dad and I shuffled our way out to his black Suburban. Dad hoisted me up into the leather seat and buckled my seatbelt for me. I opened my glazed eyes and looked at him.

"You were right, Chunky," Dad said as he stared at me.

"I was?" I asked with confusion. "About what?"

Dad chuckled. "Dean does have a killer smile."

I smiled at him and closed my eyes before drifting off to sleep.

13. Father, Daughter Chat

When I next opened my eyes a new day had dawned. But the new day didn't make the previous one disappear. I lay in bed and quietly stared up at the ceiling. I dreaded today. I hated yesterday but I was really not looking forward to today. I had a pretty good feeling I would be getting some quality Dad-time today whether I wanted it or not. We also had to go to the precinct and sign the police statement.

I yawned and stretched but I did it as quietly as I could. I wasn't ready to face my dad just yet, for a multitude of reasons. My mind replayed the moment in the Suburban just before he had buckled me into my seatbelt and shut my door. I groaned silently. That memory was just one of many.

I thought further back to the altercation with Chad. In the light of day, the entire episode didn't seem as menacing. It hadn't exactly been fun but it could have been so much worse, especially as Chad had been drinking. I didn't think he had been in very much control of his actions. Not, I immediately thought, that that excused Chad by any means. Drunk or not he had been out to provoke last night, provoke exactly what I wasn't sure, but he had definitely been looking to score off of me. Now if I could only figure out why.

Who knew, I thought, flipping over onto my side and staring

out at the sunny day beyond my window. Maybe Chad didn't need a reason to be an ass, I thought. Maybe he liked being one and last night was how he got his kicks. But he had seemed so angry with me just as he had been the entire past week. And when Chad had kept throwing Dean up to me, it was almost as if he was jealous—and angry with me for that jealousy.

None of it made sense, I thought as I watched puffy white clouds blow slowly along the skyline. I could hear birds singing and the wind lightly blowing, but none of that could drown out my troubled thoughts or my memories of last night.

It really didn't make any sense, I repeated silently to myself. Not Chad's anger or his petty taunts or his throwing me into the swimming pool. His, 'Maybe you need to cool off,' comment floated around my mind. I remembered having to repeat that to the police officer with my dad standing there, not saying a word. I inwardly cringed at the memory. A part of me couldn't help but worry that my dad might be thinking that maybe I had done something to provoke Chad.

A knock sounded at my door. I whipped my head around on my pillow and watched as my bedroom door slowly opened.

"I thought you might be awake," my dad commented as he walked in.

"Just for a few minutes," I said, staring at his face and trying to read his expression. I wanted to gauge his current mood, but his face wasn't telling me anything. He just looked like Dad, maybe a little more tired than usual. That observation made me feel worse.

"How are you feeling this morning?"

"Surprisingly good," I told him with a smile. "Things don't seem so bad this morning." I assured him. I was determined to be as positive and untroubled as I possibly could. I didn't want to worry my dad anymore than he obviously already had been.

"Good," my dad approved. "I'm sure it was a scary experience, and I'm glad you're dealing okay with it. Sometimes stuff like that can dramatically affect a person's life and I would hate for this to have done that to you."

I shook my head at him. "I wouldn't let it," I told my dad with certainty. I'd meant it last night when I'd said that I wasn't going to be a victim.

My dad grinned at the stubborn look on my face. "That's my girl! So what do you feel?" Dad quizzed me as he sat down on the empty half of the bed and lay back on the spare pillow beside mine, with his hands locked behind his head.

Dr. Phil time I thought to myself, but I really didn't mind it too much. I needed to sort it all out and since Peanut was banned from calling me for the rest of the weekend, Dad would have to do. Not to mention, I didn't think he was going to give me much choice in the matter. He was looking mighty comfortable and not a bit ready to move which meant I'd better start talking.

"Confused," I finally answered, turning my head on my pillow and glancing over at him before I turned back to stare at the ceiling. "I mostly feel confused. And angry," I quickly added.

"The anger I get," Dad said as he also stared at the ceiling. "I think that's pretty normal. Chad basically attacked you last night. You may not be hurt. You may not even have a bruise to show for it, but it was an attack nonetheless and anger is a very natural response when someone threatens you."

I nodded my head. What Dad said made sense.

"So let's talk about the confusion," Dad said, turning his head to look at me.

I turned my head to make eye contact with him. "I guess I'm confused about a lot of things but the question that keeps running through my mind is: Why? *Why* did he do it? *Why* does he seem to be so mad at me? *Why* is he picking on me? *Why* did he sneak into a party last night and single me out?" My voice dwindled away and I turned my neck and once again stared up at the ceiling. "Just *why*?" I whispered in finality.

Silence reigned for several moments. Except for the ticking of my dad's Insignia watch and our breathing, nothing else could be heard.

"What's going to happen to Chad?" I finally asked, flouncing over onto my side and facing him.

Dad had turned his head back to contemplate the ceiling and his eyes remained glued to the white plaster as he answered. "A patrolman will go to his home once we've signed the papers."

"He'll be arrested?" I asked with surprise, propping myself up onto my elbow so that I could look down at him.

Dad's eyes quickly met mine and he shook his head no. "It will be like a warning. The patrolman will talk with Chad's parents, apprise them of the situation and basically, *hopefully*," Dad emphasized with a lift of his left brow, "it will scare the crap out of Chad."

"Oh," I said, plopping back down onto the bed. "I think I'm glad about that," I said with a frown. "I wouldn't have wanted this to get him into serious trouble. He made a mistake. A *huge* mistake," I quickly clarified. "But everyone deserves a second chance." I looked over at my dad. "Does that make me sound weird or like a masochist or something?" I asked with a frown.

"What?" Dad asked. "Having compassion for your fellow man despite what they might have done to you?"

I nodded my head at him in silence.

Dad sat up so that he could look down at me, and I could tell by his body language that he felt what he was about to say was very important.

"No," Dad finally answered back with a shake of his head. "Not at all. It makes you compassionate and understanding and forgiving. It also makes you the daughter I raised you to be," he finished with an affectionate tap of his finger to my nose.

"Hmm," I murmured with a smile. "Sounds like a certain someone is wanting a little praise of their own," I teased.

"It wouldn't go amiss," Dad quipped with a wink.

I giggled.

"Feeling better, now?" Dad asked.

It took me a second to realize it, but I was. Talking with him had helped me shuffle and organize all the chaotic thoughts I'd had racing through my mind when I'd woken up this morning.

"I do believe I am," I told him. "Dr. Phil ain't got a thing on you, Dad."

Dad placed a quick kiss to my forehead and flashed me a crooked grin, before getting up off of the bed and heading toward the bedroom door. "Go ahead and get showered," he told me as he paused at the door. "We'll go to the police station and sign the paperwork and get that over with. The sooner we do, the sooner someone can be sent out to Chad's home and have a long talk with him and his parents."

"Okay," I agreed readily. I wanted to get the whole thing over with.

"And one more thing," Dad added looking at me with a serious expression on his face. "I want you to stay as far away from Chad as you can. I don't care what you have to do, but you stay away from him. For some reason it appears he's decided to use you as his whipping post and as far as I'm concerned he's gotten as close to you as he's going to get. He can find another whipping post for his issues."

"What issues?" I asked him suddenly remembering his last night's comments about knowing Chad's dad. "Is there something you know, that I don't?"

Dad looked back at me without answering which was answer enough. "You just stay away from him. If he tries to talk to you or approaches you, walk away. If you can't get away; if he grabs you again, scream fire! We understand each other?"

I quickly nodded yes. "But what about classes?" I hurriedly asked him with some trepidation. I didn't want my dad to think I was arguing with him because nothing could be further from the truth, but Chad and I sat beside each other in U.S. History. I couldn't exactly make that change happen on my own.

"What about classes?"

I quickly explained the situation. "That won't be a problem," my dad immediately dismissed. "I planned on having a meeting with your principal on Monday morning to explain the situation to him. I'll make sure any and all seating arrangements that need changing are changed."

My eyes opened wide. "You plan on going to school and telling the principal about this?"

Dad nodded his head and looked at me as if I'd asked a very stupid question. "I most certainly do."

I sat up on my bed and shook my head at him in confusion. "But why? It's not like what happened, happened at school, you know. The principal can't discipline him for that."

Dad just looked at me. "Don't think I don't remember what I heard last night, Chunky. Chad's been tormenting you at school since school started on Monday. But he crossed a line last night. It's my job as your father and a man in blue to make sure that the authority at your school is aware of the potential for trouble. Especially," he added, "because it involves *my* daughter."

"Wow!" I commented in awe.

"Wow what?" Dad asked, looking at me as if I was crazy.

"Just wow," I said, with a shake of my head and shrug of my shoulders. "You've just kind of turned into commando Dad and I'm a little overwhelmed, is all."

Dad didn't smile as I'd intended him to. If anything he looked even more serious than before. "This isn't a joke for me, Chunky. Last night was something that shouldn't have happened to you. You could have been a little more honest with me about what's been going on with Chad. I could have been a little more responsible and not let you go to a party that wasn't going to have any parents. The Scott's could have been a little more responsible by not letting their boys have a party with no chaperone. Peanut could have been a little more responsible by meeting back up with you at the party like you both had agreed to. And so on and so on and so on... You get my drift?"

I nodded my head.

"I'm not blaming you, or the Scott's or Peanut or even myself," he insisted. "I'm just saying we all dropped the ball. I don't plan on dropping it again. Feel me?"

"Yes sir," I answered quickly. I'd been deceived earlier by my dad's easy going manner. I was only now realizing that he was taking what happened last night even harder than I was. He felt as if he'd missed some detail that could have warned him. I could tell, that no matter what he said, he felt partially responsible for what had happened last night, and that made me feel guilty. It wasn't like I'd been totally honest with him. I'd hid everything that Chad had done to me from him. How could he anticipate an attack if he didn't even know there was a potential threat out there? Though in all honesty, I would have never guessed in a million years that Chad would have done what he did.

"Dad, you know this wasn't your fault?" I quietly asked from my spot on the bed.

Dad ran his hand over his baldhead. "Yeah, I know but it still shouldn't have happened," he grunted and I knew there was nothing I could say that would alleviate the sense of parental guilt he was feeling.

Still I had to try. "I don't blame you," I told him. "Chad is responsible for what happened and if anyone else is next in line for blame, it should be me. I could have told you about Chad."

Dad nodded at me adamantly. "Yeah you could have," he instantly agreed, before adding, "And you *should* have. I hope you learned a valuable lesson from all of this."

"Of course," I readily agreed out loud, though I secretly hoped that there would never be another incident such as this where I would have to utilize such a lesson. Once was more than enough for one lifetime.

14. Dead Wrong

"Oh my goodness, Chunky. How are you?" Peanut gushed as soon as I was inside of the car. "I was so mad at your dad when he said I couldn't call you. Then both my mom and dad agreed with him and said everything could wait until Monday. I've been dying! Haven't I Butter?" she asked, looking over at him.

Butter grinned at me through the rearview mirror. "I don't know if she's been dying or not, but I sure can tell you that she's been *killing* me!" he said with a wink. "Seriously though, you okay?"

"I'm fine," I assured him, before turning to Peanut who looked as if she didn't believe me. "Really," I told her. "I'm perfectly all right. The whole thing was scary and extremely disorienting but I'm feeling a great deal better. Almost completely recovered," I reassured her.

"Were you in trouble with your dad?" Peanut asked with a grimace.

I shook my head no. "He wasn't happy about the whole thing and he didn't like that I hadn't told him how Chad had been acting but if anything, he was blaming himself."

"Why?" Butter asked with a frown. "What could he have done to prevent it?"

I rolled my eyes at him. "I haven't got a clue as to why. I think it's mainly because he's my dad and also a police detective. Somehow to him, that equates complete omnipotence and should give him Superman capabilities. I tried to tell him that I didn't think he was to blame at all, but I don't think he was listening. He was more focused on making sure something like this doesn't happen again.

"Well, I can't argue with that," Butter muttered. "And as long as I'm around it won't," he added adamantly. "Chad better think twice before coming around you. He won't find it so easy next time, I can assure you."

"Butter," I tried to caution. The last thing I wanted was Butter getting into trouble on my behalf.

"No Chunky. I'm serious. I'm not going to be looking to start any trouble but you better believe I'll be paying attention to whether he is."

"And if he is?" I asked

"And if he is, then I'll be there to stop him. Not only me, but Dean, David, and Eric, too. There's no way in the world we're going to let him get away with the kind of crap he pulled on Friday night. No way!"

"Go Butter!" Peanut cheered him on.

I rubbed at my temple with my fingers. I could feel tension tightening the muscles around my eyes. "Look," I said. "I don't want anyone getting into trouble over this. I'm going to avoid Chad from here on out. My dad is going to the school today to speak with the principal. Everything should be dealt with and will die down if *everyone* just lets it. Okay?" I practically begged.

Butter turned into the school parking lot and parked in our spot. Stopping the car he turned around as far as he could in the compact confines of the car and looked at me. "Chunky, you know I'd never do anything to hurt you, right?" he asked.

I nodded. "I know Butter."

"Well then, you should know that by the same token, *I*

cannot sit back and let somebody else hurt you. It's just not in me. And I won't. Just like I wouldn't let anyone mess with Peanut. So where I can promise you that I won't start anything with Chad, I simply can't promise not to defend you. Understand?"

I huffed out a laugh. "I understand. I don't have to like it, but I understand."

"Good!" Butter said, turning back around in his seat. "We better get going. I don't know what kind of gossip will be floating around out there but I don't want to look like we're hiding you out in here. It'll be best if we go out there and pretend nothing happened. We have to at least show them you have nothing to be embarrassed about or ashamed of."

I groaned. "Maybe I'm not as okay as I thought I was," I confessed to both of them in a small voice. "I don't want to do this."

A loud knock sounded at Butter's window and all three of us jumped in our seats. We all looked at each other and laughed before looking toward the sound. The laughter had dispensed much of the tension that had begun filling the small car.

"Hey guys!" Butter said as he opened the door and started to get out. "What's up?" I could hear him ask as I opened my door and slid out. I'd yet to raise my eyes from my feet to meet anyone's gaze.

"Good morning," a familiar voice said from above me as a large, waving hand was thrust into my line of vision.

After the briefest hesitation, I laughed at myself, feeling stupid. I lifted my head and smiled into Dean's eyes. "Sorry," I apologized. "Just some residual side effects but they're gone now. Want to try again?"

"Nah," Dean said still smiling. "I like how this one is going so far. I don't want to take any chances you know. If we start over you may run away. You never know how those beastly residual side effects will affect a person, you know."

I rolled my eyes at him. "Do boys really say *beastly*?" I teased with my hand on my hip and my head tilted enquiringly.

Dean pretended to look offended for a few seconds before he chuckled at himself. "Now I'm feeling embarrassed," he groaned covering his face with his hand. "I can't *believe* I said beastly."

I started to laugh as did everyone else who'd apparently been listening in on our conversation.

"Oh yeah you did man!" David said, giving him a small shove while laughing at him. "And I don't plan on forgetting it or letting you forget it anytime soon," he warned.

Everyone continued to laugh and tease each other as we made our way toward the quad. Though I joined in with the laughter and the talking, I was still very much aware of the looks and whispers that were going on around us. Though not enjoyable, it didn't appear to be as bad as I thought it would.

"You okay?" Dean whispered in an aside to me.

"Mmm hmm," I murmured in answer.

"That's my girl," he responded, causing me to whip my head around in his direction. Had he just called me his girl? Dean smiled down at me and winked but he didn't say anything else. My mind whirled at the possibilities.

We joined some friends and we all stood around talking. A few people mentioned the party but it was only in general. No mention of the incident was made and I began to suspect that the guys had made some calls over the weekend to clear things up on my behalf. My heart ached at the thought of these big boys protecting me. I remembered what Butter had said a few minutes ago in the car and I smiled to myself. This day was going to be perfect.

"Oh my gosh!" someone suddenly exclaimed. A hush fell, to soon be replaced by loud gasps and louder whispers. I looked around to see what everyone was talking about. At first I assumed it had something to do with me but when I overheard, "I wonder who gave him the black eye?" I knew it didn't. It was kind of weird, but I knew immediately whom everyone was talking about and my eyes swept the quad searching. I saw him a few seconds later. It was Chad. Chad: with a grossly swollen black and purple right eye.

"Oh my God," I whispered, swinging around to look for Butter. "Please tell me you didn't do this?" I pleaded with him. Only a few minutes ago I had been practically glowing from his over protectiveness, now I just wanted Butter to snatch all of the things he had said back if it meant he'd done this.

Butter looked at me confused, before understanding dawned. "You think I smashed Chad's eye?"

I nodded yes at him before quickly shaking my head no. "I don't know, Butter. That's what I'm asking," I finally was able to say.

"Calm down, Chunky," Butter said grabbing my hands to still their shaking. "I would love to have been the one to give Chad that shiner but it wasn't me. I swear," he added when I still looked upset. I glanced around at the other guys before back at Butter. I finally started to regain control. Obviously the other guys wouldn't have done that just for me. I began to breathe a bit easier.

"You didn't do that to him did you, Dean?" David suddenly asked in a low voice.

I whipped my head around in disbelief as I looked at David. "Of course not," I said. "Why would he?"

David continued to stare at Dean without saying a word. Dean gave David a short sharp twist of his head as if he was answering no, but I gave them no more of my attention. I turned back in the direction Chad had been walking but he was no longer in sight. My stomach flopped as I contemplated who could have done that to Chad. I became queasy at the possibilities.

The bell suddenly rang and everyone began walking towards their classes. I didn't move but stood staring off into the direction Chad had disappeared.

"Hey?" Dean murmured from beside me. "We need to get going if we don't want to be late for class."

"Yeah, of course," I quietly agreed as we started walking but I couldn't help but glance back.

"You okay?" Dean asked with a frown.

I could understand the frown. "I know you probably think I'm crazy considering everything Chad has done to me, but he didn't deserve that Dean. Did you see his eye? It's a mess."

Dean looked down at me as we continued to make our way to class. "You're a sweet girl," he finally murmured with a twist of his lips. "And yeah, I personally think you're wasting your time worrying about Chad. It's the very least that he deserves for manhandling you and scaring you like he did," Dean insisted as we paused outside the classroom door.

Before I could walk inside Dean suddenly reached out and grabbed a lock of my brown hair, twisting the stands around his index finger. He stood there for the briefest of seconds, staring at the strands wrapped so trustingly around his finger before releasing them. He smiled as he watched the strands bounce back into their habitual place. "You're a really sweet girl," he repeated again, before extending his arm out, indicating that I should precede him into Biology.

I walked into class in a daze. I had the strangest feeling that Dean had been about to say something different but for the life of me I didn't have a clue as to what. The way he had been staring at me had made me thinking that he was going to say something more personal, but that he had changed his mind at the last minute. I spent the rest of the period trying to imagine what it could have been.

By the time U.S. History rolled around, I had almost forgotten about Chad and his black eye. Though Mr. Smith reassigned my seat as soon as I walked into the room, I knew I would see Chad when he walked in. I waited in tense anticipation for him to show up.

I dreaded the moment but for some reason I was perversely

anticipating it as well. Probably because of his eye, I told myself but mostly because I hoped and prayed that somehow he would be sorry for what he had done and that miraculously his animosity would be gone and I wouldn't have to worry about him or his intentions anymore. The bell rang signaling the beginning of class but Chad still hadn't shown up. Chad still had not shown up forty minutes later when class let out.

The rest of the school day crept by. There were many whispers and innuendos about Chad and his eye. Many people gave me speculative looks as they passed me in the hall. I didn't pay attention to any of them and I didn't see Chad again.

Dean on the other hand was a different story. He stayed by my side from lunch till the end of the day. I made a point of being very careful about not mentioning Chad again. I didn't want Dean to think I had some kind of warped fixation on Chad. I didn't want Dean to look at me like one of those poor women who love men who treat them like crap, because it wasn't like that. I didn't like Chad that way. I really didn't like Chad at all and never had. But it didn't mean I couldn't see with my own eyes that something bad was going on in his life. My dad had practically confirmed it this weekend by not saying a word in response to my question about Chad's dad.

When the sixth period bell rang, I was in no rush to leave class. Today had been extremely long and exhausting. I yawned and stretched my arms above my head.

Dean turned around in his seat and caught me mid-yawn. I quickly lowered one of my arms to cover my mouth. "Oops! Sorry," I mumbled around my hand.

"Not a problem," Dean chuckled.

I looked over to where the other guys on the team stood in a circle talking and waiting for Dean. "I think they're waiting for you," I told him, cocking my head in their direction.

"I know," Dean said. "I told them I need to talk to you for a second first."

"Oh?" I asked. I was curiously excited. This was a first.

"Yeah," Dean said, looking down at his right hand that was rubbing at the material of his shorts in what looked like nervous circles. "I never got the chance to tell you how sorry I was about Friday night."

"Oh," I said again this time sounding much less excited.

"I don't want to bring back bad memories," Dean said obviously misunderstanding my tone. "I just needed to tell you that you shouldn't listen to a word Chad says, because he's wrong you know," Dean whispered, standing up and hooking his book bag over his shoulder. "Dead wrong," he murmured quietly, before walking away to join his friends and leaving the classroom.

"Oh!" I said again into the silence left behind by his departure. "Oh my!"

15. Sit Back and Enjoy

I walked as if in a daze towards my locker. Had he just...? Was he saying...? Did he mean...? One question after another flashed through my mind, but I couldn't concentrate long enough to find any answers.

"You look funny," Peanut said as way of a greeting.

I turned to her with a blank look on my face. "I feel funny."

Peanut's cheerful face instantly turned to a look of concern. "Are you sick?" she asked, reaching up to put the back of her hand to my forehead.

I slapped it away and rolled my eyes at her. "I didn't mean I was sick, you idiot."

"Well, what did you mean?" she said, slapping me back in retaliation.

I looked over at her. "Okay, hypothetically," I started to say but Peanut interrupted me.

"Hypothetically?" she scoffed. "As in we're going to talk science here or...?" she added. "As in you're trying to con me into thinking we're talking about someone else when in fact we're about to talk about you, hypothetical?"

I rolled my eyes at her again and laughed. "You know me to well."

125

"Only because that's how you act when you're embarrassed or if it's something kind of private. I thought you'd have figured out by now that I can see right through it. For goodness sakes, Chunky," Peanut laughed at me. "Even Butter knows it."

I blushed. I could remember a conversation or two that I'd had with Butter in the past that had gone a little something like the way Peanut had just described. In my stupidity I thought I was getting advice from Butter without the embarrassment of having to have him know that the advice I sought was actually for me. And here I'd thought I was being so creative and sneaky.

"Thanks for finally telling me," I muttered in embarrassment.

"Sorry," Peanut said unrepentantly.

"Yeah, I can tell."

"So anyway," Peanut quickly changed the subject. "What's this "hypothetical" question?" she asked, holding her fingers up in the air and imitating quotation marks.

"Let's wait until we're in the car," I said, looking over my shoulder. I definitely didn't want anyone overhearing this conversation.

"Hmmm, sounds mysterious and very, very intriguing." Peanut said while waggling her eyebrows at me.

"Mmm hmm. That's me," I agreed. "Mysterious *and* intriguing," I finished while hurriedly grabbing what books I needed tonight for homework and putting the ones I didn't back into my locker. I wasn't about to take any of the mason-like weights that the school called books home if I didn't have to.

Slamming the locker door shut and resetting the combination back to zero I hooked my book bag over my shoulder and headed toward the school parking lot. Peanut and I stopped a couple of times to talk with a few people. Thankfully, I didn't appear to be the main topic of discussion. All in all, today hadn't been as bad as it could have been. Ironically, I owed that small favor to Chad and his black eye.

Eventually we made it to the car. Peanut unlocked the doors and we climbed inside. Rolling down the window I leaned back into the seat and sighed. It had been a long day.

"So what's up?" Peanut asked, as she twisted the key in the ignition and started the car.

I finally started to speak as she pulled out of the parking space. "Today, right at the end of sixth period," I clarified. "Dean..."

"Dean, what?" Peanut asked, looking over at me.

"This is going to sound lame," I laughed trying to find the right words to explain. "Dean just usually says bye and leaves with some of the guys on the football team. They head straight for practice." I looked over at Peanut and she nodded her head at me in understanding. "So, *today*," I stressed. "He didn't immediately leave. He turned around to talk to me, and he told me that he'd told the guys to wait on him because he needed a few minutes to talk to me."

"Sounds promising," Peanut cut in with a sly smile.

I smiled in remembrance. I had thought the same thing at the time. "Exactly what *I* thought," I admitted out loud to her. "But then he started talking about how he hadn't had time to tell me he was sorry about what had happened at the party."

"Oh," Peanut said in a deflated tone, sounding so much like I had when Dean had said it to me that I started to laugh. When Peanut gave me a look that said she was starting to question my sanity, I laughed all the harder.

When I finally stopped laughing, I shook my head and apologized. "Sorry about that but your reaction was just so funny. It was practically identical to mine and it tickled me."

"So what did you say to him?" Peanut asked with a glance in my direction. Apparently she was going to ignore my odd sense of humor.

"I think I said oh, twice." I finally answered. "Real academy award winning stuff," I mocked myself and my more than inept reply to Dean.

Peanut giggled. "So is that it? Is that the entire conversation?"

"No," I answered shaking my head and remembering the last thing Dean had said to me. The thing I was finding so hard to interpret. "No," I said again. "He stood up, you know, and gathered up his stuff and I felt let down, thinking he was leaving and that all he'd wanted to tell me was that he was sorry. Poor little Chunky, you know. But then... then he told me that he hoped I didn't listen to the things Chad said because Chad was wrong..."

Peanut whipped her head to look at me, before looking back at the road. "No way!" she screamed. "He said that to you?"

I smiled back at her, pleased by her reaction. "Not only said it," I confirmed. "But he repeated it in this really quiet, serious voice. He said that Chad was 'dead wrong'."

"Oh my gosh!" Peanut squealed in delight. "I so wish I had been there to hear that."

"It felt pretty great," I admitted. Then I frowned. "But what do you think it means? Or does it mean anything at all?" I asked in a rush. I looked over at Peanut for guidance.

"First and foremost Chunky, it means Dean's a pretty smart guy and that you should listen to his advice."

I rolled my eyes at Peanut. "That's not what I meant and you know it," I scolded her.

"But I'm right nonetheless," she immediately quipped back, before continuing on. "Second of all, I think it's kind of promising. Not because he said it the first time, but because the way you say he said it the second time. That sounds personal, you know what I mean? As if the first time he was telling you as a friend to let it go, but the second time he was telling you as a boy who truly believes it."

Peanut's words literally gave me chills up and down my skin. She'd put into words what I was feeling but couldn't for the life of me make sense of.

"What do you think I should do?" I asked Peanut with a frown.

"I wouldn't do anything, Chunky. I think that if I was you, I'd sit back and enjoy Dean's friendship and attention."

"But what if we're wrong about all of this, Peanut? What if he was really just being nice?"

"Then no harm done," Peanut responded quickly. "You and I will be the only ones to know that you thought any differently and you won't tell a soul and you know I'll take that information with me to the grave. So," Peanut said throwing her hands up into the air, "no harm done."

Suddenly, Peanut glanced over at me with a sly smile playing on her lips. "Just out of curiosity, what were *you* thinking you should do about it, because I really can't see you making the first move with him? Or any guy for that matter."

I blushed. I hated it, but it happened anyway. Shyness had that effect on people like me. "I didn't have a plan." I answered after a moment. "Because you're right, there's no way *I* would have or could have ever made the first move. I just wanted to know what you'd say, oh wise one."

"Smart girl," Peanut approved in a haughty tone and jaunty toss of her head. I refused to comment. I simply shook my head at her and looked out the window.

We road on in silence for a few minutes, her driving and humming along to a song on the radio and me, staring blankly out the window still thinking of Dean and rehashing in my mind everything he had done and every word he had ever spoken and... Then it hit me. There was actually something he had never said to me, or more precisely, never called me, and that was Chunky.

My mind stretched back over the countless encounters we had had at school and at the party and after the party and I couldn't think of one time that Dean had addressed me as Chunky. As far as I could remember, the one and only time I'd ever heard Dean say, Chunky was the day we first formally met in the cafeteria. And even then, when he said it, I could remember thinking how uncomfortable he appeared using it.

"May I ask you something?" I suddenly burst out to Peanut with an unexpectedness that shocked even me.

Peanut's head whipped around at the force of my voice. "What's wrong?" Peanut asked sharply, her head turning back towards the road as she continued to drive.

"Okay," I said briskly while I turned in my seat to face her more directly. I discovered that both of my hands were squeezed into fists, and that I was digging my fingernails into the palms of my hands. In an effort to relax, I lay them down on my thighs, before straightening out my fingers so that my hands lay open and face down on denim.

"What's gotten into you, Chunky?" Peanut asked, as she observed my restive movements.

"Okay," I repeated with a deep breath. "I know I'm probably reading way too much into this, but I have to ask you something. Just now, I realized something. I realized that I can't recall Dean ever calling me Chunky."

"Yes he has," Peanut immediately and automatically contradicted me from her side of the car.

"When?" I shot back at her. "Other than the very first day when we first introduced ourselves, he has never called me Chunky. Or any other name come to think of it," I assured her. "And even back then, I remember thinking how he seemed to stutter when he said my name," I told her, watching her as she mulled this over. "Think about it Peanut. Can you remember hearing Dean ever call me Chunky?"

I waited a few minutes while Peanut mentally replayed the various encounters we had had with Dean since we had met him. Her eyebrows crinkled and her brow lightly wrinkled as eventually she came to the same conclusion I had.

"I can't believe it, Chunky," she finally gasped out, looking over at me briefly with wide eyes. "You're right. I cannot remember Dean calling you by name. Not one time," she admitted with a shake of her head. "How could we have *not* noticed this? What even made you realize it just now?" she asked, turning to look at me again as we sat stopped at a red light.

I shrugged my shoulders at her in answer. "It just kind of came to me. I mean," I said with a slight blush, "I was sitting here replaying everything with him in my mind and the things he's said and done and it hit me! Just like that."

We stared at each other until a car horn honked.

"All right. All right," Peanut grumbled, breaking eye contact and glancing into the rearview mirror at the car behind us. "I'm going already," she murmured to the impatient driver with an apologetic wave of her hand before driving off. As she drove she kept throwing little looks my way.

"What?" I finally asked her.

"Exactly," she said enigmatically. "What? What do you think it means?"

I shook my head at her. "I haven't got a clue, Peanut. Not a clue. But for some reason I do think it means something. I just don't know what, and I'm afraid I'm letting wishful thinking interfere with my usual realistic view of life."

Peanut shook her head as she pulled the car into my driveway then parked the car. "If it helps," she offered, turning in her seat a little to look over at me, "I think you're right. There's something significant about him not calling you Chunky, but I just don't know what that significance is."

Nodding my head at her in agreement, I gave her a lopsided grin. "I'm starting to wish I hadn't had this revelation because there's nothing pleasant about having a revelation if you can't figure out what it means. It tends to create more questions, rather than answer them, and I already had a ton of questions to begin with!"

"I agree," Peanut said. "But hang in there," she encouraged. "I think things with you and Dean have the potential to take off."

"So what about you and David?" I asked, cocking my eyebrow at her. "You haven't said much about him."

Peanut grimaced. "I don't think there is going to be a David and me. He's really nice to me and I think he's great, not to mention pretty hot, but I'm not sure anything will come of it."

I grimaced at Peanut. "I'm sorry. I know you were pretty excited about getting to know him."

Peanut shook her head at me. "It's okay really. I think I jumped the gun a bit. He's new and cute and single. I just had new guy fascination, you know what I mean?"

I grimaced again. "Do you think that's what I'm feeling?"

Peanut immediately shook her head no. "Not at all, Chunky. There's definitely something there. What becomes of it remains to be seen."

I thought about that for a second then nodded my head at her. "I can live with that," I decided.

"I thought so," Peanut said, waving goodbye to me as I got out of the car.

I headed into my house and grabbed a bottle of water from the fridge. After taking a long swallow, I recapped the bottle and laid it down on the counter. I sighed to myself. I needed to start a load of laundry before I started on my homework. I had a lot to do tonight—of both.

Sometime later, the ringing of the telephone startled me. I glanced at the clock on the wall to see what time it was. I was shocked to see that it was past six. My dad would be home any minute, I realized, as I reached to pick up the telephone, and I hadn't done anything about dinner. Hopefully he'd bring take-out.

"Hello," I answered in an abstracted tone. I was trying to think of what I could whip up for us to eat if he didn't.

"Chunky!" Peanut said, breathless with excitement. "You are not going to believe what I just found out!"

"What?" I asked with confusion, taking the phone away

from my ear and rubbing at my abused ear. "And please talk softer. You almost busted my eardrum."

"Oops," Peanut giggled. "Sorry!"

"Forgiven, now tell me what all of the excitement is about," I ordered, more than a little excited at the possibilities.

"So okay," Peanut started in a thankfully, softer voice. "Butter came home from practice tonight and you aren't going to believe what he said happened," she repeated.

"Well, I might if you give me a chance and finally tell me," I insisted in an aggravated tone. Peanut could be so exasperating when she got like this.

"When Chad showed up for practice and the coach saw his eye, he told Chad that he couldn't play him like that. Coach told Chad that he would have to ride the bench this game and that Dean would not only start the game, but he would be finishing it, too."

For a second I was thrilled by the news. I was so happy for Dean. But in the next instant I couldn't help but wince for Chad. As if the black eye wasn't bad enough, now he couldn't play at all. I knew some people would think he deserved it, and a part of me, if I was being honest with myself, did as well. But another part of me, the part that felt there were some really bad things in Chad's life that were making him act as badly as he was, hated this second, possibly more crushing blow.

"Chunky?" Peanut demanded in my ear. "Did you hear me? Chad's benched and Dean's getting to play the whole game!"

"I heard you, Peanut and that's great news for Dean. Did Butter say how Dean reacted when the coach told him?"

"Butter said that half of the team cheered, but that Dean acted real humble and cool. Butter said that Dean actually walked over to Chad to talk to him about it, but that Chad stormed off of the field."

"I bet," I muttered imagining exactly how Chad would be taking news like this. Chad hadn't been acting exactly pleasant lately. I didn't imagine his attitude would be much improved after this.

"Butter said Chad acted like a real jerk and that he couldn't even believe Dean tried to talk to Chad to begin with," she paused for a significant moment. "You know," she paused again. "After what he did to you on Friday," she explained in a rush.

"I remember, Peanut," I said with a roll of my eyes at her needless reminder. "I don't think I'm likely to forget anytime soon."

"I guess not," she responded meekly, before bouncing back in enthusiasm. "But can you believe it? If you ask me, Chad is getting his just desserts."

"You know what they say about Karma," I commented.

"Yeah," Peanut giggled. "It'll come back to punch you in the eye."

I couldn't help it. I laughed. "That isn't funny," I tried to say to her around my giggles.

"Yes it was," she said unrepentant.

"Okay, it was," I agreed, before quickly adding. "But it was wrong. Just plain wrong."

"Maybe," she finally admitted. "But I'm not about to apologize for it. A joke or two at Chad's expense is what that boy needs, if you ask me. He needs someone to take him down a peg or two then maybe he won't be so quick to pick on other people."

"Like me," I muttered, remembering all of the things Chad had said and done to me. And he hadn't cared who heard him. He liked to play to an audience.

"Most importantly you," Peanut confirmed.

"Still, Peanut," I said more firmly. "I'm fine with Chad being banned from the game. I'd be fine with him not being able to play for the rest of the year because that would mean Dean would be playing. But I can't condone his being punched or agree with whoever did it. Did you see his eye?" I asked her.

"That wasn't any little light tap. Whoever hit him wanted to really hurt him and I can't be happy about that."

"You actually feel sorry for Chad, Chunky?" Peanut asked with surprise. "Even after what he did to you?"

"Yes. No. Maybe," I finally answered in confusion. "I just can't help but wonder about who did it and why." I wasn't going to mention to Peanut that I thought the culprit might be his own father. I wasn't about to start gossip like that as it was only speculation on my part. I had a feeling Chad could be a lot more unpleasant to me than he already had been if he thought I was passing a rumor like that around about him.

"Well, you're a bigger person than I am, Chunky."

I grinned. "I thought the name Chunky pretty much gave that away," I joked to her. It was definitely time to change the subject.

I could hear my dad's Suburban pull into the drive. I grimaced as I glanced at the clock again and realized I had been on the telephone a lot longer than I'd thought.

"Look, my dad is home and I haven't done a thing about getting dinner ready," I urgently whispered. "I need to at least be pretending to look through the fridge when he walks through the door."

"He'll know what you're trying to do, Chunky," Peanut warned with a giggle. "I don't know how your dad does it but he always knows things."

"Tell me about it," I muttered back. "See you tomorrow," I hurriedly added and hung up the phone. I could hear his footsteps right outside the kitchen door and I made a mad dash toward the pantry. Macaroni and cheese sounded like it had possibilities.

I glanced over my shoulder as he walked inside. Much to my delight he was carrying a Subway bag. He held it up for my inspection.

I nodded in appreciation. "But how did you know I hadn't already started making something?" I asked with curiosity.

Dad smirked at me. "I'm a detective. I know lots of things."

16. Dealing with Dad

The next few minutes were spent gathering glasses from the cabinet and chips from the pantry. I filled my dad's glass with his habitual milk while I poured some iced tea for myself.

"You need to drink more milk," Dad chastised me when he noted what I was *not* drinking.

Here we go again I thought in aggravation. We had this conversation like ten times a month. "I hate milk, Dad. It makes me sick to my stomach and you know I take calcium supplements."

"You like ice cream," he stubbornly insisted.

"I know and I don't know why milk bothers me and ice cream doesn't. It's probably one of those, what do they call it?" I asked facetiously. "A scientific anomaly?"

"That's very funny, Chunky."

I giggled. "It actually kind of was," I said, before giggling some more.

Dad gave me one of his famous looks. "You're quite the comedian tonight, Chunky. I take it that means school didn't go so bad today?"

I swallowed the bite of tuna sub I was chewing before

answering. "Not too bad for me," I agreed. "But I can't say the same for Chad."

"And what kind of day did Chad have?" Dad asked with curiosity.

"The kind where you show up at school in front of all your friends and classmates sporting a very ugly black eye," I answered, before taking another bite.

"That *is* a bad day," Dad agreed, nodding his head and devouring half of his twelve inch chicken teriyaki. "Anyone we know claiming responsibility for Chad's new condition?" he questioned after he swallowed.

I shook my head. "Not that I'm aware of or at least, not as far as anyone is admitting to," I clarified, popping a sour cream and onion baked chip into my mouth.

"So you think you know who it was?" Dad asked me with seriousness after wiping his mouth with his napkin.

I nodded at him. "I have my suspicions but it's not who *you're* thinking," I answered with just as much seriousness.

"And how would you know who I was thinking?" Dad asked with curiosity as he started in on the other half of his sub.

"I don't," I answered honestly. "But I figured your top suspects were Dean or Butter."

"And you don't think it was Dean or Butter?" Dad asked around a bite of his food.

"No," I said adamantly. "I know it wasn't them." I took the last bite of my sub.

"Why so sure?" he quizzed.

"Because I asked them, and they said no. I've known Butter for so long I would have known for sure if he was lying to me," I said after I swallowed.

"And Dean?" Dad asked. "What makes you so sure it wasn't Dean?"

I shrugged feeling weird answering this one. "I just am. That's not Dean's way."

"Look Chunky, that's *any* guy's way if they feel they've been pushed too far," he warned. "Don't put Dean in a pair of shoes he can never completely fill. You'll only end up hurting yourself if you do. And you could end up hurting him, too."

"Well, I still don't think Dean did it," I repeated. "And yes," I added, before he could say anything. "I did listen to every word you said. It's just not Dean."

"Then who do you think did it?" Dad asked as he finished the last bite of his own sub.

I looked up at him from beneath my lashes. I wanted to see his reaction when I told him my suspicions. "I think it was his dad."

Dad was wiping his mouth again as I told him. His hand hesitated for only a hundredth of a second but it was still a hesitation, nonetheless. My suspicions grew stronger that my dad knew more than he was willing to say. It appeared Dad wasn't the only one in the family with detective skills such as hunches.

"Why do you think it's his dad?" he asked me in a manner that, in my opinion, was a little too nonchalant.

"Because of something you said on Friday night," I quickly responded while I continued to watch him carefully.

Dad's eyes widened at my response but all he said was, "And what did I say, exactly?"

"You intimated that you were familiar with Chad's father through work and as Chad's dad isn't on the force in any way, it made me think you'd met him on the other side of the bars, so to speak," I concluded.

Dad stared at me for a long minute. "You got all of that from what I said on Friday night?"

"Yep!" I admitted with a touch of pride and a cocky tilt to my head.

"Don't look so smug. I haven't confirmed anything."

"And you're not going to," I concluded for him. "I get that, Dad. As far as I'm concerned the least I know the better. It's just that I feel kind of bad for him, you know. Peanut doesn't understand how I can feel sorry for him after the way he's treated me, but I can't seem to help it."

"You told Peanut that you think Chad's dad hits him?" he asked me with disapproval.

"Oh no!" I quickly denied. "We were talking about Chad being benched for Friday night's game because of his eye, and she was saying she was glad, and I was saying I didn't mind that he didn't get to play football, but that I couldn't condone what had been done to him..." I was explaining when Dad sliced his hand through the air to cut me off.

"Back up," he said. "What are you talking about, now?"

"The coach told Chad he couldn't play at all on Friday because of his eye," I explained and understanding dawned in my dad's eyes.

"I see," he said nodding his head. "So Peanut doesn't understand why you would feel bad for him."

"Sort of," I agreed.

"You don't have feelings for Chad do you Chunky?" Dad suddenly asked into the silence.

I thought I'd bite my tongue off in shock. "No!" I practically screamed. "What in the world makes you ask me that?" I cried. I was absolutely appalled that my dad could even ask me such a question.

"I was just asking," he replied with his hands up in mock surrender. "My next question was going to be if you had feelings for Dean?"

"Dad!" I screamed again, throwing the balled up Subway wrap at him. "What's gotten into you tonight? First you ask me an insulting question like whether I like Chad, of all people, *Chad*! And then you completely blindside me by asking me about my feelings for Dean. Just what has come over you?" I screeched.

Dad threw his hands up in exasperation. "Heaven only knows," he said with sarcasm. "I mean ask yourself why I might *possibly* want to know if my daughter has a thing for a boy with obvious troubles and not to mention a terrible temper. Or... Or *why* I might be interested in the possibility that she has a crush on a jock that has just made the starting position of quarterback for his high school football team? I mean really, Chunky. What *could* I have been thinking?"

"Sorry," I mumbled, feeling chastened and ashamed of myself. I could tell that I'd hurt my dad's feelings even if I hadn't meant to. "It's just—Chad, Dad? Really? I never liked Chad before this school year. I can assure you I'm not the Stockholm syndrome kind of girl."

"That's good to hear," Dad said in approval as I paused to take a breath.

"Though you shouldn't of had to," I couldn't help but flash back at him in response. "As far as your question about Dean," I murmured quietly, looking down at the table and tracing the ring left on the table from my cold glass. "It's just embarrassing talking to you about him."

"Why?"

"Because you're my dad!" I answered, looking up at him as if he was crazy.

"And because I'm your dad I don't get to talk to you about the things that make you happy?" he asked. "That doesn't really seem fair to me, Chunky."

I stared at him long and hard. I couldn't tell how serious he was being. I thought most parents, or in my case, parent, knew that at some time in their kid's life there came a time when that said kid wouldn't want to share everything. It wasn't done as a punishment to the parent, or at least not by me. It was just private and personal. But now, looking at it from his point of view, it probably did feel like a punishment. I came to a sudden decision. I just *so* hoped I wouldn't regret it later.

"Okay," I said as I slammed my hands down onto the table. "You can have three questions a week about boys. *Any* boy," I clarified.

Dad stared back at me contemplatively. "Is that an in depth question or an in general question?"

I smiled. "One in depth and two in general."

"Okay, "Dad agreed while nodding his head. "And can I ask this question at anytime during the week or do I have to ask all three at once?"

I thought about that for a minute. I was sensing that this question was a trick question, but I couldn't figure it out. Unable to find the invisible trap, I finally answered, "Anytime."

Dad smiled a wolfish smile.

"What?" I asked suspiciously with a frown.

"You just agreed that I could grill you with three questions before a date or three questions after a date. Anytime," he disclosed while continuing to grin. "Either way, I win!" he finished as he threw his trash into the trashcan and walked out of the kitchen.

As I watched him walk away I had the sneakiest feeling that I had just been *royally* conned.

"Dad!" I yelled after his retreating back. "That's not fair. You tricked me into that."

"A deal's a deal!" he yelled from the other room.

"But..." I started to yell back but stopped myself before I turned to outright begging.

I got up from the kitchen table and flung my own trash into the garbage can before wiping the crumbs off of the kitchen table. I grumbled my way through the entire process. I couldn't believe that I had been so gullible. I'd let him dupe me with his pitiful little speech about how it wasn't fair that he couldn't be more involved in his teenage daughter's life. All the time he was trying to con me into giving him carte blanche access into that life. And I fell for it, I thought, as I stomped my way to my bedroom.

A little while later, I was still fuming when suddenly I had to laugh. The joke was really on my dad after all. It wasn't like I had a boyfriend or a life to speak of. He could ask all the questions he wanted, but I'd make sure he'd be bored by the answers.

I woke up the next morning still thinking about the trick my dad had pulled on me. I was pretty sure it was the lowest thing he had ever done. Payback, they said, was like a female dog. I hoped I was around when she peed on his shoes.

I dressed for school in my usual uniform---jeans and t-shirt---only this t-shirt was sleeveless and bared a fair amount of cleavage. I'd never worn anything like it. Peanut had urged me to buy it while we were back-to-school shopping. For some reason, today felt like just the right day to wear it.

I stood for a long time in front of my mirror, staring at my reflection. A voice inside of me kept telling me to take it off and put on something that showed a little less skin. But then there was Peanut's voice, the one I remember from inside the dressing room. *Her* voice kept urging me to wear it. That voice had said, "If you've got it, flaunt it." And I had it all right, I thought as I looked at my exposed neckline. I had it in abundance.

I finally compromised by keeping the shirt on but I slipped a lightweight pink jacket on over it. It was the kind of jacket that was more for looks rather than warmth. I also had an idea that it might be the only way I'd make it farther than the kitchen. I wasn't so sure my dad was ready to admit that I had cleavage yet, let alone allow me to share the view with others.

In the kitchen I downed my glass of orange juice in record time. I had taken so long in getting ready this morning that I was running behind. I glanced at my dad as he walked into the kitchen.

"I forgot to ask you last night," I said as I rinsed out my glass. "What happened with the principal yesterday?"

"Nothing much," he answered with a shrug. "I told him what had happened. I asked him to keep his eyes open, and I asked that he make it clear to all of your teachers that you were not to sit near Chad. I assumed that was taken care of?" he asked with eyebrow cocked.

143

"You assumed correctly," I informed him. "Not that it made a difference in U.S. History yesterday. Chad cut class."

Dad shrugged at me. "I'll be the first person to admit that Chad's got some tough things to deal with. But he better *deal* with them and leave you alone. I can be compassionate, but I refuse to be blind. He's had his one chance with you, Chunky. The next time he won't get off so easily."

"Don't get me wrong Dad," I said, hooking my book bag over my shoulder. "I completely agree with you. Chad can't treat me, or anyone for that matter, like his own personal whipping post. But you didn't see his face yesterday, Dad; all purple and swollen. If you had, I don't think *you'd* think he'd gotten off so easily."

"Possibly not," he acquiesced, but I had the feeling my dad's view on the whole black eye thing was a lot like Dean's. They saw it from the male perspective and evidently the male perspective involved fists.

"Boys!" I muttered under my breath, making my dad laugh.

I headed toward the kitchen door when I heard Princess pull into the drive. "You be careful!" I said as I turned around to give him a glare that said I meant business. All this talk of black eyes and fists and fighting made me remember the line of work my dad was in. Those kinds of things could very well happen to him today.

"Always!" came the expected response.

I was about to shut the kitchen door when suddenly he called my name.

"Yes?" I asked, looking at him while my mind was already halfway out the door.

"Nice shirt."

17. Recruited by Mrs. Drysdale

The ride to school was spent rehashing yesterday's football practice and Chad's benching by the coach. It was more than obvious that Butter was happy with the results. I didn't argue because I felt the same. Not about the black eye, because that was just barbaric, but the rest of it.

I'd realized sometime last night while I lay in bed trying to go to sleep that though I felt compassion for Chad, it was the kind of compassion I would have felt for a stranger on the street who had been hurt. That didn't mean it extended into total forgiveness and absolution of his past actions. It was really two separate things and I was glad I could understand that now. My dad asking me yesterday if I liked Chad had been more than my mind could handle, and it had tortured me until I could finally understand my feelings.

Compassion did not mean automatic forgiveness. Knowing someone was being abused by another did not make them your friend. Understanding why someone hit out at you didn't make it okay. Understanding all of these things gave me a better perspective and insight into myself, and how I viewed and dealt with others. It was a good lesson.

I spent most of the ride listening to Butter and Peanut banter back and forth. I smiled on several occasions, as one would strike a spark off of the other. They tried to drag me into the middle of it a few times, but I had learned long ago to never involve myself in one of their squabbles.

As Butter pulled into the parking lot he murmured, "Dean and David are behind us."

I resisted the urge to turn around and look. I'd thought about walking up to Dean today and hugging him in congratulations, but I had talked myself out of it in no time. I was a hugger or at least I thought I was. I knew I *wanted* to be. But self-consciousness and feelings of ineptness always held me back. I couldn't imagine anything worse than going in for a hug only to have that person stiffen up on me. I couldn't put myself out there enough to risk that kind of rejection. Especially with Dean.

I'd also always tried to imagine what the person I was hugging would be thinking about me. Would they feel how soft I was, instead of firm? Would they compare me to their skinnier friends? Would they think they had to stretch their arms out really wide to get them around me? All kinds of really stupid questions popped into my mind when I thought about hugging a guy. The questions would then put an end to any desire I might have had to hug that person to begin with. (Hence, I didn't plan on hugging Dean in congratulations this morning after all.)

I climbed out of the car to find Dean standing there waiting for me with a big grin. "Did you hear the news?"

I gave him my best smile back. Oh man, I thought to myself, why couldn't I just hug him? "I sure did," I finally answered. "It's awesome! Congratulations!"

"Thanks," Dean replied still grinning. "You're coming to the game to watch us play, right?"

"Of course," I instantly responded. "I wouldn't miss it for the world."

"Hey man!" Butter cut in. "Don't get too excited about that. She comes to see *me* play. Always has, always will."

I laughed over at Butter. "You know you're my hero, Butter."

I looked back at Dean and was surprised to catch a funny look on his face as we watched Butter, but when he saw me looking at him he quickly smiled again.

"Is something wrong?" I quizzed.

"No," Dean instantly replied with a shake of his head.

I had the feeling he wasn't being completely honest with me, but other than calling him a liar and demanding to be told what the problem was I had to let it go. That was surprisingly harder than I thought it would be.

I kept watching Dean as we reached the quad and our other friends. He smiled and joked with everyone and accepted the good wishes he got from everyone around him as they learned about him getting the starting quarterback position. After about five minutes I decided to stop worrying about whatever had been bugging Dean because it obviously no longer was.

"Chunky!" Mrs. Drysdale chimed in her tiny voice. I inwardly cringed. This was obviously going to be a repeat of the first day of school. "Oh Chunky, dear?" She called again, taking her impossibly tiny steps in my direction. I decided it would be better to meet her halfway. At least that would prevent her from screaming Chunky out ten more times.

"Yes, Mrs. Drysdale?" I asked as I approached her, almost tripping over nothing in particular. I stumbled a few feet before I caught myself. A quick glance around showed that no one appeared to notice, either that, or everyone was just so used to my klutziness that they no longer paid as much attention. I guess my entertainment value had decreased over time, I joked to myself.

"Chunky, dear," Mrs. Drysdale started speaking, halting my meandering and inane thoughts from getting out of hand. "I need your help Friday morning before classes start. I want to clean out that old musty closet in the back of the library."

"Sure, that shouldn't be a problem." I told her.

I really wanted to ask her what she thought I could possibly help her with, but couldn't bring myself to do it. Mrs. Drysdale just really liked me for some reason, which meant she usually picked me every time she had a chore that needed doing or something needed fetching or cleaning or carrying. Basically whatever she thought up during the week. But a lot of those times it was something that usually required two people and not one. Unfortunately though, Mrs. Drysdale always included herself as part of the two, which of course meant I ended up having to do everything by myself.

I looked up as Dean suddenly appeared by my side.

"Well, hello there dear boy," Mrs. Drysdale acknowledged him. "I don't believe I've had the pleasure of meeting you."

"No Mrs. Drysdale," Dean said extending his hand. "I'm new here. My name is Dean Scott."

Mrs. Drysdale lightly grasped his hand and patted the back of it with her other one. "It's nice to meet you, too," she said, clearly impressed by his manners. "And actually," she continued looking from Dean to me, and then back again. "You're just what I need. Chunky is going to help me pull a few things out of the old library closet on Friday morning, but I believe the task may be a bit too much for her to do on her own. I don't suppose you'd mind helping her with that, would you?"

Dean quickly looked over at me before turning back to Mrs. Drysdale. "Of course not," he promptly answered.

"That will be wonderful, dear boy. Just, wonderful. Now if you two will meet me thirty minutes before class in the library, we'll get started then."

Dean and I immediately agreed to meet her in the library at the designated time and a few seconds later, Mrs. Drysdale toddled off.

"Oh crap!" I suddenly said, smacking myself in the forehead.

"What?" Dean asked, looking at me with a frown.

"I ride to school with Butter and Peanut. I don't want to

ask them to come to school so early just for that. Oh well," I decided. "I'll just have to ask my dad to bring me."

"I can pick you up," Dean offered slowly.

I looked at him. Of course I wanted to immediately scream, yes, but I hesitated. Those self-esteem issues were raising their ugly heads again. "Are you sure you don't mind?"

"Of course not," he murmured looking directly at me. It felt almost as if he was trying to say something else but for the life of me I couldn't figure it out. Then again, maybe I was just, once again, reading too much into it.

"Well, if you're sure," I said awkwardly. "Then yeah, that would be great," I finished then quickly gave him the directions on how to get to my house.

The bell picked that minute to ring. I waved to Peanut, before Dean and I started walking to class. I didn't trip once.

The rest of the day passed uneventfully. That was except for U.S. History. That class was a little stressful for me at first. Chad showed up, but he was wearing glasses so I couldn't see his eye. It also meant that I couldn't tell if he was looking in my direction either. After the first glance, I didn't look toward him again and after about fifteen minutes I began to relax again.

The end of sixth period also provided a little glitch in what was an otherwise average day. After the bell rang, Dean turned around in his seat to talk with me. As we chatted about nothing really, I glanced towards the door and noticed that the guys from the team weren't waiting for him. I turned back to tell Dean when he volunteered the information on his own.

"I told the guys to head on to practice without me and I'd catch up with them."

"Oh," was the only thing I could think of to say. What was the appropriate response with something like this, anyway, I asked myself? I didn't want to assume that he was saying that he wanted to spend more time with me. I was not about to make an assumption like that. I knew the old saying about what assuming did; it made an ass out of me and *me*.

"Yeah," he finally said. "It always seems like I have to rush off. I thought it would be nice to walk you to your locker for a change," he astounded me by saying. "Because," he went on to tease, "I worry about what kind of damage you could do to yourself when you're on your own."

"Hey!" I said punching him lightly in the arm, shocking myself at my own playfulness. "I am quite capable of walking myself to my locker without anything happening, thank you very much!"

Of course, in the next instant I had to eat my words. In my quest to show Dean how capable I was, I grabbed my book bag from the wrong end and all of my books went flying out. As I quickly bent over to begin picking up the mess, my head encountered Dean's in a resounding crash that had me seeing stars for a few seconds.

"Oh," I groaned in pain while my hands grasped at the stinging spot. A few seconds passed while I tried to absorb the initial onslaught of pain.

"I'm so sorry. Are you hurt?" I finally gasped out, trying to look at him through the tears that had instantly appeared in my eyes when our heads had collided.

"Mm… yes, I think so," he muttered as he rubbed at the front of his head with his hand. "You were saying?" he added with grunt.

I knew I deserved that so I kept my mouth shut. Instead, I bent over again, this time making sure that Dean wasn't doing the same and began picking up my scattered books. "I am really sorry," I mumbled in embarrassment.

Dean reached for a few of the books that had fallen in another direction. While he did, he began to laugh softly to himself.

"What's so funny?" I grumbled in continued embarrassment.

"If I say *you*, will you be mad?" he asked around his laughter.

"Maybe," I answered with caution.

"Then I think I'll plead the fifth," Dean answered with continued laughter. When he finally seemed to regain control of himself he grabbed his book bag and mine as well and stood up. "Let's go," he said as he began walking towards the door.

When we got to the door he held his hand out to indicate that I should walk out in front of him. I thought I heard him murmur something about a guy couldn't be too careful, but when I turned around to look at him suspiciously, he gave me an innocent grin.

"What?" he asked a little too ingenuously.

I decided he deserved a free pass considering I had almost given him a concussion. I had to start laughing then. It *was* pretty funny, embarrassing as all get out, but definitely funny.

Dean started to chuckle as soon as I did, and we walked toward my locker together like two laughing hyenas. Despite the pain and large bump on my head, I hadn't had so much fun in a long time.

Of course the laughter for me lasted until I caught sight of Chad glaring at us from across the quad. That stopped my laughter immediately. I looked away from him.

"What's wrong?" Dean quickly asked when he felt me stiffen beside him.

"Nothing," I answered immediately. Boys and fists instantly came to memory. There was no way I was talking. "Nothing," I answered more calmly.

I looked at Dean and pasted on a smile for him. Not that I found smiling at Dean a difficult thing to do. In fact, it was usually a very easy and natural thing for me. Only it wasn't so easy when I knew I wasn't being honest with him. Dag gone it, I thought to myself in disgust, I really didn't like Chad.

18. When Hairy Met Chunky

Peanut was already standing at my locker when Dean and I walked up. "Hi!" she smiled at Dean with a wiggle of her fingers. She then turned to me with eyebrows raised. I pretended not to notice the significant eyebrow lift or the unspoken question she was asking. I had no intention of explaining anything to her until she and I were alone.

"Hi," I simply answered back and proceeded to work the combination to my locker. Dean stood propped up against the locker beside mine and watched as I deposited and extracted various books and notebooks. I tried to act as normal as possible throughout the entire process.

Peanut was standing quietly on the other side of me taking everything in. I was pretty proud of her. I knew how hard it must have been for her to keep her mouth shut. I'd have to remember to thank her later.

Grabbing the last book I needed, I stuffed it into my book-bag and slammed my locker door. Dean reached out unexpectedly and grabbed the heavy bag from me.

"I'll carry this for you," he said easily, as if nothing abnormal or strange was happening at all.

Peanut looked at me from the corner of her eye, before cutting them to Dean and resting them pointedly on my book bag that was now slung over Dean's very strong shoulder. I gave her the tiniest of shrugs, saying without words that I wasn't sure what was going on either. Of course, that shrug couldn't also tell her that whatever it was, I liked it a whole bunch.

Instead, as nonchalantly as possible, I looked up at Dean and smiled. "Thanks. That can get to be pretty heavy some times."

"My pleasure," he smiled back down at me. "Ready?"

I realized Dean was probably in somewhat of a hurry, as he had to prepare for football practice, so I quickly answered, "Sure."

I thought about offering to carry it myself so that he could go ahead and leave for practice, but for the life of me I couldn't bring myself to do it. I wasn't sure what was happening here. I knew what I wanted it to be, but want and reality weren't always interchangeable. So, instead of telling Dean I'd carry it, I decided to enjoy the moment while I had it. Lord only knew how long it would last.

Peanut, Dean, and I made our way down the short hallway. I couldn't help but wish that it would be a lot longer than it was. "What are you going to be doing tonight?" Dean asked.

"Mostly homework." I answered automatically while my brain scrambled for something less mundane to say and not having much luck. "I also have to finish a poster for Mrs. Drysdale," I suddenly remembered aloud, "and I've only done half of it."

"A poster?" Dean asked with curiosity.

I blushed. "I don't know if you were in the quad on the morning of the first day of school, but Mrs. Drysdale hunted me down to ask me to help her with some art work," I explained.

"Art work? You mean like drawing pictures?" Dean asked with interest.

"Yeah!" Peanut jumped in and answered for me. "She's great. Mrs. Drysdale always asks Chunky to help her create new designs for her displays in the library. Chunky's really good."

"Impressive," Dean commented. Then he frowned for a second. "So you're like her jack of all trades?" he joked.

I started laughing, but Peanut didn't get the joke so I began to explain. "Mrs. Drysdale cornered Dean and me this morning to help her clean out some things from that old closet in the back of the library. Dean's just commenting on the fact that she doesn't just ask me to draw but clean up... and pick up... and put up..."

Dean laughed. Peanut nodded her head in agreement. "That's why I'm always careful not to be standing beside you when I see Mrs. Drysdale in the vicinity. Nine times out of ten I know she's going to ask you to do some little project for her and I don't want to get suckered in to helping like you always are."

Dean grinned at Peanut and lifted up his free arm. "I guess that makes me a sucker, too!"

Peanut laughed at him. "The first time doesn't count because you didn't know better. But now you do. So if it happens again then yeah, you're a big ole lollipop." We all laughed.

In no time, we arrived at Butter's car. Peanut stopped at the driver's door and Dean walked with me around to the passenger side. Once the doors were unlocked, Dean reached across me and opened the door for me. Impressed more than I could say, I murmured a thank you, before climbing into my seat. As soon as I was seated, I reached out so that Dean could hand me my book bag.

"Thanks again," I told him with a smile as I looked up at him.

"No problem," he returned with a shrug of his shoulders and a little grin that had me holding my breath at the sheer beauty of it.

Peanut started the car and snapped on her seatbelt, jarring me back to reality and the realization that I had been staring unabashedly for long moments up into Dean's face like a love-sick fool. I felt the heat pour into my cheeks.

Dean however, appeared not to notice anything unusual and cocked an eyebrow at me and asked, "See you tomorrow?"

I nodded my head. "See you tomorrow," I promised.

Dean winked and with a last wave and a "watch out" he stepped back away from the car while simultaneously swinging my door shut with a solid thud.

I smiled and waved at Dean as he stood there watching Peanut and me pull out of the parking space.

"Don't say a word. Not one," I whispered through my lips, trying not to move them. "Wait until Dean can't see us anymore," I warned. "Or so help me Peanut, I'll smash you until only creamy is available."

Peanut giggled through her closed lips but she refrained from actually smiling or laughing outright. Actually she stayed completely quiet until after we left school grounds. But that was as far as it lasted.

"You've been holding out on me, Chunky!" Peanut accused.

I looked over at her and shook my head in denial. "No I haven't," I defended myself.

"So you're just saying that out of the blue, Dean decided to walk you to your locker and then carry your book bag for you to the car?" she paused with significance, before tacking on, "Like a boyfriend would?"

I nodded. "That's exactly what I'm saying," I confirmed, before quickly clarifying, "Everything but the boyfriend part. I didn't say that. That's all you!"

I started grinning really big at Peanut and I couldn't seem to stop. "Oh my gosh!" I gushed. "Do you really think he was acting like a boyfriend?"

"Well, I haven't had many," Peanut admitted. "But that's kind of how they act in my experience."

My smiled slipped. "But he hasn't asked me to be his

girlfriend," I moaned. "We don't really talk about things like that; boyfriend, girlfriend stuff. He doesn't even have my phone number!" I finished bleakly.

The euphoria of moments ago was quickly dissipating as reality returned. Not that I wasn't still happy about the time I spent with Dean, but trying to figure out what it all meant was an entirely different matter. A part of me really felt as though Dean was flirting with me. It really seemed that he liked me as more than just friends. I mean I hadn't noticed him carrying any other girl's book bag nor had I seen him hanging around another girl's locker.

Yes, I had to admit I'd seen him talking to girls. He'd been talking to Emilee the other day in the quad. And though they'd seemed pretty friendly at the time, I really hadn't seen him talk to her since.

Peanut's sudden and piercing scream ceased all existing thoughts except the paramount one of what the heck! My body was thrown forward against the seatbelt in a somewhat painful manner as the sound of tires screeching filled the confines of the car. The car skidded for what felt like hundreds of feet, but was probably no more than five, before shuddering to a stop, throwing my body back against the seat.

Long moments passed. The only sound was the sound of our harsh breaths as we gasped aloud in shock and fright.

"Are you okay?" Peanut squeaked out as she sat without moving and stared straight ahead.

"I think so," I muttered as I rubbed at my chest where the seatbelt had cut into me. "What happened?" I asked, looking over at her. "Why did you stop so suddenly like that?"

"There it is!" she screeched, as she unhooked her seatbelt with trembling fingers. Her hand floundered with the handle of her door before it finally connected, and she pulled the handle back and opened her door. In seconds she was scrambling out of the car as I sat by watching her with my mouth hanging open in disbelief.

"Peanut!" I yelled after a few seconds of wit gathering and mind clearing. I struggled briefly with my own seatbelt before the clasp finally released. When I opened my door I practically fell out of my side of the car. I walked over to where she stood on the side of the road, staring into the tall, brilliantly green and wildly growing brush.

"Peanut!" I demanded this time. "What in the world are you doing? You could have killed us!"

"I almost killed *it*!" she answered, as she turned around toward me with a worried expression on her face, before turning back to stare with wild eyes into the overgrown vegetation.

"Killed what?" I asked with confusion. I hadn't seen anything. I *still* didn't see anything. Then again, I reminded myself, I *had* been more inwardly focused at the time.

"The dog," she gasped, still searching the side of the road. "Or at least I *think* it was a dog," she said with a deep frown of worry.

A tiny yip sounded from the right of us in response to Peanut's voice. The sound came from close by. And it did sound like a dog. My eyes searched the tall swaying grass. Another tiny yip sounded about a yard away from where I stood. Taking a few steps forward, I glanced over and down and burst into silent laughter or as silent as I could make it.

"Is that the dog?" I asked Peanut, pointing to show her where to look.

Peanut walked softly over to where I stood. She didn't want to frighten it into running away. After staring at it for a few seconds, she finally whispered with a funny look on her face, "Don't dogs have hair?"

I knelt down and watched the dog sniff its way towards me. The grass was so high that I couldn't tell if it was a boy or a girl. But by the way it acted; it was obvious that it was very shy and timid. I slowly knelt down as it approached me. As it took its time deciding whether it was going to trust me or not, I took my time studying it. It really was a very *odd* looking creature.

It had dark gray skin with pale pink splotches. The only hair on its body was on the tips of its ears, toes, and tail.

"Hi there," I murmured to it as it came closer. I slowly extended my hand toward it and it sniffed at my fingers delicately, before taking a swipe at them with its tongue. "It's nice to meet you, too," I told it in response to its friendly salute.

"It doesn't have hair," Peanut repeated from her spot beside me.

I glanced up at her. "You've already said that," I teased, before glancing back down at the tiny dog at my feet. "I think it's a Chinese... something hairless. I've seen pictures, but I can't remember what they're called." The dog, who I could now tell was a male, was sniffing at my feet and hands and it appeared he liked what he smelled.

"Ugly?" Peanut guessed.

"Hey! You'll hurt his feelings," I scolded Peanut. "He's not ugly. He's interesting," I clarified while reaching out with my hand slowly to pet his hairless body. I didn't want to startle him.

"Interestingly ugly," Peanut refuted. "I don't care what kind of slant you try to put on it, Chunky. That dog's just ugly."

"So ugly he's cute?" I offered as a compromise.

Peanut laughed. "If *you* say so."

"Come here little guy," I said as I gingerly picked him up into my arms. "It's a boy," I told Peanut as I glanced over at her. "He doesn't have a collar and he looks pretty skinny. What do you want to bet that he's gotten himself lost or that someone threw him out on the side of the road? This is no mutt, Peanut. A dog like this isn't a stray."

"That's terrible," Peanut ground out. "If you don't want the responsibility, then don't get it to begin with."

"I couldn't agree more," I murmured as I rubbed the ugly little guy's tummy. There's no way in the world I was going to admit to Peanut that I found him ugly, too. Because he *was* so ugly he was cute. "Dad and I haven't had a dog since Pilot died," I continued absently as I stroked the fluffy head. "We just haven't been ready to replace him."

"Oh no!" Peanut exclaimed. "Please don't tell me you plan on replacing that wonderful golden retriever with this hairless rat?" she demanded

I looked at her as I stood up with the scrawny animal in my arms. He was starting to shiver and I could hear his tummy rumble in hunger. "Maybe," I answered abstractedly, as I walked back toward the car with him in my arms. "But first I'd have to put up flyers in case he *is* lost and not dumped. He may have owners out there searching for him. I couldn't keep him without finding out for sure."

Peanut rounded the car and hopped back into the driver's side. "I haven't seen any flyers Chunky that would indicate someone was looking for him. I bet he was dumped.

I nodded my head sadly as I snuggled the hairless pup deeper into my arms. I was shocked at how surprisingly smooth he felt despite the lack of fur. "He most likely was dumped but I'd still have to make sure. I wouldn't feel right otherwise."

Peanut started the car and drove the short distance to my house at an incredibly slow pace. It was obvious that she hadn't quite recovered from her earlier fright.

"So I take it I'm dropping him off with you?" she questioned as she parked the car in my driveway.

"I think you are," I answered her with a smile. I then looked down and smiled at the *him*, in question. "You want to go home with me?" I asked him. The tiny tongue shot out again and lapped at my chin. I looked up at Peanut. "I guess that means yes!"

I gathered my book bag and slung it over my shoulder, before securing the dog in my arms, so that he would feel safe. I could feel him start to shiver again.

"Chunky?" Peanut called out to me, as I was about to shut the car door.

"Hmm?" I was too busy making faces at the dog to look at Peanut.

"Aren't you forgetting something?" she quizzed.

Suddenly I remembered Dean and this afternoon and all the unanswered questions that had been circulating in my head. "How could I have forgotten?" I gasped. "I have no idea what he's thinking. Do you think I should ask him?"

Peanut frowned at me in confusion. "Oh I think you'll know exactly what he's thinking when he sees that, Chunky," Peanut said as she pointed to the dog in my arms.

I frowned back at her. "How would Dean see the dog, Peanut? That doesn't make sense."

Peanut giggled. "I was talking about your dad you idiot, not Dean. I was asking you, if you'd forgotten about your dad and what he would say about this... this... dog?"

"He has feelings too, Peanut!" I admonished her and her continuous insulting of my new four legged friend. "And I'm not worried about my dad. He told me to let him know when I was ready to get a new dog. I'll just tell him I'm ready and I've already picked one out."

Peanut smirked at me. "You make it sound really simple, but I can't see your big bad daddy walking a froo froo dog like this on a leash. I think it's probably against some detective rule or something that says he can't own a dog unless it weighs at least a hundred pounds and that when it barks it actually barks, and not yips like this one does."

I rolled my eyes. "My dad won't have a problem. You'll see," I assured her. "As long as no one claims him, we'll be keeping him. I better start thinking up names," I rambled to myself as I waved goodbye to Peanut and walked with my new pet into his new home.

This first thing I did with him when we went inside was to get him some fresh, cool water. The poor thing lapped it up greedily. He'd obviously been dying of thirst. The second thing I did was to take him outside into the backyard. Thankfully our backyard was fenced in so I didn't have to worry about him running out into the street and getting hurt.

He pranced and explored and peed on about every tree and bush he could find. Evidently he liked what he found and was marking this place his.

As he ran around chasing bugs and dried leaves, I reviewed a dozen different names in my mind. I even called out a few, trying them out. He didn't respond to any of them. None seemed appropriate.

Glancing down at my watch I realized it was later than I thought. Picking the literally, skin and bone, animal up, I carried him back into the house with me. I set him down on the carpet and was about to search for an old blanket when the kitchen door suddenly opened, sending the once docile animal into a frenzy of barking. I ran toward the kitchen door. I cringed at the uproar the tiny dog was making and shuddered to think what my dad was making of all the chaos. This was definitely not the good first impression I wanted the dog to make.

"What in the hell is that?" Dad roared at me over the bombardment of the loud, frenzy barks. "And where is his hair?"

And just like that, with my dad's furious words, my new pet was christened.

"That's Hairy, Dad," I said with a grin. "He's our new pet."

19. Don't Forget

Dad didn't say anything for the longest time. He kept swinging his eyes back and forth, from Hairy, to me, and then back again. I couldn't gauge what he was thinking or feeling or if it was good or bad. I waited quietly for some kind of response. Finally it came.

"Pet what?" he asked with sarcasm, allowing his eyes to land on Hairy and stick.

"Dog, of course," I told him as I picked Hairy up to give him a cuddle. His little body was shaking and shivering. "Oh Dad you scared him!" I accused with a frown.

"I..." Dad paused with an incredulous look on his, "scared *him*? He tried to bite me!" he bellowed in total affront.

"No he didn't," I immediately refuted. "I was standing right here and he did no such thing. If anything, you should be impressed by his gallant show of defense on my behalf," I argued. "It's not his fault that he didn't know who you were. Now that he's met you, I'm sure he'll greet you more calmly in the future."

"The future?" Dad asked, with a little tilt to his head that always indicated that I may not like what he was about to say.

"Yes," I answered not as confidently. "I want to keep him," I told my dad, before quickly qualifying my declaration. "I want to keep him if I can't find his owners."

"I see," Dad said. "And at anytime did you ever ask yourself whether you should consult me or not? Your father," he clarified. "You know, the man that owns this house. The same man that's supposed to make the final decisions in said house. You know," he paused for terrifying effect, "this particular man that I'm talking about?"

I swallowed. My dad didn't usually intimidate me. I knew he was mainly bluster. But I had a feeling that I'd misjudged his entire reaction to me keeping this dog. I hated to admit it but Peanut had been right. Dad was most definitely not thrilled with our new pet.

"Sorry," I tried to placate him. "I really didn't think you'd mind. You've always told me that I could have a new pet whenever I felt ready. This one practically fell into my lap— well actually, almost into the front of Butter's car," I quickly amended, before continuing. "I didn't stop to think that you wouldn't want him."

"Chunky," Dad groaned. "That's not a dog, it's a rat. A very ugly rat."

"It's a dog, Dad. I still haven't had time to look up his breed name but I know it's something like Chinese hairless or something like that. He's supposed to *not* have hair."

"Dogs should never, *not* have hair," Dad suddenly declared.

Said dog was currently sniffing my dad's shoes. He must have liked what he smelled because suddenly he laid down with his tiny head propped on top of the toes of my dad's shoe and promptly went to sleep.

I laughed softly. "Well, you may not like him but he's definitely decided that he likes you." I laughed harder when I caught the expression on my dad's face. If I didn't know better I would have thought he was blushing.

Dad bent over and scooped the sleeping dog up into his arms. "He really is an ugly beast."

"But may I keep him?" I asked after a second.

Dad sighed deeply. He looked up at me and finally said, "On three conditions."

"And those conditions are?" I decided to ask, before simply agreeing. Last night with this unscrupulous man had taught me caution if nothing else.

"Fast learner," he approved reading my mind. "But seriously, you make flyers with the dog's picture and my cell phone number. If somebody calls and can prove that he's theirs, then we give him back."

"Definitely," I instantly agreed to the first condition. "That goes without saying. And what is the second condition?" I prompted him.

Dad looked down at the freakish looking animal in his arms then looked back up at me. "That you are responsible for taking him out on the leash for walks. I won't mind letting him out into the backyard to do his business, but I refuse to walk him out on the streets."

I smothered a laugh. There was no point in poking a grouchy bear. "That's not a problem, either."

"Third," he said with a stern expression. "And by far this is the most important condition of all, you," he said pointing his finger directly at me, "Never, ever, tell the guys at the precinct about this. I'll never live it down."

I burst into laughter. The look on his face was comical and what he said was practically what Peanut had said earlier, almost verbatim.

The dog woke up with a start at the sound of my laughter. He immediately began wiggling his tail and trying to lick my dad's wrists. With one last glance at the dog, Dad stuck him out toward me. "Keep your mouth shut," he warned with a last disdainful glimpse at Hairy, before he walked out of the kitchen.

I looked down at Hairy cradled in my arms and bent down to nuzzle his little nose. "Don't worry buddy. He's going to learn to love you."

I decided the smartest thing to do for the rest of the night was to lay low. I also thought I'd better hurry and prepare Dad some kind of dinner. A fed man was a happy man, or at least I'd heard some very old black and white commercial once advertise. For tonight at least, I hoped it was true.

I spent that night alternating between loving on Hairy and thinking about Dean. I decided to put off making Mrs. Drysdale's posters until the weekend. Instead, I told Hairy about my day and the excitement I'd felt when Dean had acted so attentively. Hairy didn't have an opinion either way, but he did make a great listener.

The next morning I couldn't wait to get to school. I kept wondering how Dean would act. Would it be like yesterday? I kept looking out the window for Butter and Peanut, but they never came. Dad glanced at his watch. "You better call them."

Just as I reached for the telephone, it rang. Of course it was Peanut, explaining that Princess had decided to be a drama queen this morning and wouldn't cooperate and start. "Mom said she'd take us," Peanut finished explaining and after telling me they'd be here soon, we hung up.

"Princess?" Dad asked.

"Yes," I answered trying to mask my frustration. At this rate I wasn't going to see Dean.

"Rust bucket," Dad grunted.

"Totally," I said, feeling grouchy enough about my ruined plans to agree, instead of giving my customary defense of Butter's baby.

Peanut, Butter, and I finally made it to school. I walked into first period about five seconds before the tardy bell rang. I got a glimpse of Dean but he wasn't looking my way, so he didn't see me.

The class dragged and I was anxious for it to be over with. I really wanted to see Dean. More importantly, I wanted to see how Dean acted when he saw me.

But of course, the fates were conspiring against me. Right before class was to be let out; Dean was summoned to the office. That meant I wouldn't see him until at least lunchtime.

Aggravated, I walked quietly to my next class lost in thought, which turned out to be a very big mistake. Halfway across the quad, I stumbled and bumped into the person passing me in the other direction. Off balance, I flung my arms out wide, trying to find my footing. In the process, my hands knocked against something plastic and sent it flying. I heard a curse before I felt arms grab onto me and jerk me to a stop.

"Why can't you watch where you're going?" Chad practically growled, before flinging me away from him.

I rubbed at my arms where he'd grabbed me. "Sorry," I muttered looking up at him.

That's when I realized I must have knocked off his sunglasses because he was staring down at me with only one good eye. I winced as I imagined how painful his injured one must be. The wince was my second big mistake.

"Don't pity me, Chunky girl," he snarled, before bending over and picking up his glasses. He slid them back on and started to walk off. I continued to rub at my arms and was about to turn away, when Chad suddenly stopped and looked back at me, calling my name.

I hesitated, before looking over at him. "What?" I asked with suspicion.

"Did you have a nice swim?"

I turned away without answering. Chad's laughter mocked me all the way.

By lunchtime, I was pretty much beyond the point of excitement. The entire day had been one big disappointment after another. This combined with my most enjoyable encounter with Chad; well... it had just sucked. And lunch, it appeared, wasn't going to be any different.

"What's up?" I asked Peanut as I sat down at the table. None of the football players were there.

Peanut rolled her eyes. "Coach wants the guys to go over plays for tomorrow's game while they eat lunch."

"That doesn't seem fair," I said with raised eyebrows and undisguised disappointment.

Peanut shrugged. "You know boys and their football." She leaned in closer toward me. "So has anything else happened that I should know about?" she asked with waggling brows.

It was my turn to roll my eyes. "It's hard for anything to happen when I haven't seen him all day. Between getting here late, his being called out of class, and the coach's apparent obsession with the game, I haven't even smiled at him, let alone said hello."

Peanut wrinkled her nose at me. "Sorry."

"Not your fault," I quickly assured her. "Maybe it's a sign, you know. Maybe I was reading too much into everything and this is God's way of letting me know, before I get too hurt. Maybe I've taken good manners and my liking of said manners too much to heart. Maybe I'm giving Dean grossly exaggerated chivalrous attributes because that's what I want in a guy. I'm old fashioned like that despite this being the 2000's. There's a very good chance that I've taken simple good manners and blown it up into a great love affair."

"Chunky, I don't think it's as complicated as that," Peanut declared with a shake of her head. "Not to mention, with your dad, I dare you to date a guy with no social graces. Detective Royal May wouldn't let you out the front door let alone on a date if the guy lacked something as simple as manners. No matter how the world changes, Royal May doesn't." Peanut emphasized with a hard nod of her head. "So give it time, Chunky. You guys have fifth and sixth period together. Wait and see how that goes. Okay?"

I shrugged. "Okay."

Peanut suddenly grinned. "Speaking of how things are

going; how did your dad like the new member of the May family?"

"You mean Hairy?" I asked in a dry tone.

Peanut burst into a fit of hysterical giggles. "You named that dog Hairy?" she asked, before another round of hysterics took over. A tear rolled down her cheek and she swiped at it with the back of her hand. "That is just too funny, Chunky." When she finally calmed down enough she cocked her eyebrow at me. "So how did detective Royal May take it?" she insisted on knowing.

This day couldn't get any worse, I thought as I finally confessed. "He took it exactly the way you said he would—there—satisfied?"

"Oh yeah!" Peanut sang out smugly.

"I thought you would be," I said with a sniff. I tried to look haughty and unaffected but I felt that my blush was probably giving me away.

We quickly finished our lunch and said goodbye, then we each walked to our respective classes. Despite my disappointment in how this day was turning out, I could feel a furrow of excitement ignite low in my stomach as I walked to class. I was finally going to see Dean.

The excitement didn't last long because by the time I got to class, Dean was already there and he was in the middle of a group of guys talking. They were all talking with excitement about tomorrow night's football game. I had no desire to interrupt, so I sat down at my desk and started digging through my book bag for my books. Right before the bell was supposed to ring, I felt a touch on my shoulder and a warm voice near my ear.

"Hey there," Dean murmured, as he passed by me to sit down at the desk behind mine. "I haven't seen you all day."

The bell rang then, forestalling any response I might have wanted to make. Instead, I had to force myself to focus on Spanish for the next forty minutes. However, I was never at any moment not conscious of Dean sitting behind me.

Thankfully, the Powers That Be took pity on me and the bell rang, dismissing us on to next period. I hurriedly stuffed my book and notebook into my book bag before standing up. Dean walked up close behind me as we waited for the person in front of us to clear the aisle.

"So how's your day been?" Dean asked, as we inched our way forward.

Terrible is what I almost blurted out before sanity returned. It had mainly been terrible because I hadn't seen him all day. It probably wouldn't have been too smart of me to blurt that truth out. "Okay," I finally said with a nonchalant shrug.

Dean smiled at me. "That good, huh?"

I shyly grinned back at him. "A typical school day," I answered with another shrug of my shoulders.

"Nothing exciting happened today?" he asked, as we finally stepped out into the hallway and began walking to our next class.

A mental image of Chad quickly came to mind, but I'd already decided not to tell anyone about it. Not Peanut. Not Butter. Not Dean. Not my dad. No one. The way I looked at it, Chad wouldn't have bothered me if I hadn't literally bumped into him. Not that I'm responsible in any way for Chad's behavior, but I had noticed that he'd been keeping his distance from me all week. That alone allotted him this one freebie from me.

"Nope," I finally answered Dean, before a sudden boldness took hold of me and I found myself blurting out, "Schools just boring for me without you, I guess."

Dean blinked down at me for what seemed like for ever, and as each second ticked by I wanted the ground to open up and swallow me whole. And most importantly, I wanted to take back the last 9 words I had just said. But then in the next instant the slight, questioning smile he'd already been wearing grew until both dimples were clearly defined.

"That's... umm... that's nice to hear," he said while nodding his head.

It was my turn to stutter a bit. "Well... umm... you're welcome," I breathed out surprised beyond belief by this entire conversation.

We arrived at our class and Dean stood back, allowing me to enter first. I couldn't help but think back to what I had just been saying to Peanut about how much I loved Dean's manners. He was good at those chivalrous kinds of things, like holding a door open for me or letting me walk into a room first. I know it isn't a very PC thing for me to like, being what feminism is today, but I *did* like it. I didn't think Dean was trying to tell me he was stronger than me or better than me, just because he was being courteous towards me. I appreciated the gesture and that was just a fault a woman's libber was going to have to accept in me.

We found our seats at our desks, this time mine behind his. He turned around in his seat, facing me, as the bell had not rung yet.

"I'm going to have to head straight to practice today," Dean told me and I hoped I was disguising the disappointment I was feeling. "Coach is pretty stoked about the game tomorrow and he wants to go over a few new plays."

I nodded my head in understanding. "Coach can get kind of fanatical this time of the year," I simply commented. I didn't want Dean to think I assumed he would be walking me to Butter's car again, like he had done the day before.

Dean groaned. "Tell me about it," he responded. "I've had some tough coaches before but this one is an original."

"We love our football here at Mansfield High," I said in way of apology. "Go Wolverines!" I gave the air a fist pump.

"That's good," Dean grinned. "You should be a cheerleader."

I blinked at him. Yeah, I thought to myself, like that would happen. But all I said was, "Nah, I'm too peppy. I'd be liable to kill someone." Dean started chuckling immediately. It was obvious that he got that I was referring to my habitual klutziness.

"On the other hand..." he drawled still fighting a chuckle while rubbing at the spot on his head where I had previously crashed into him. "Maybe we could use you on the football team. You could be our secret weapon," he teased.

I laughed aloud at the mental image his words conjured. "A secret, huh?" I asked with a mischievous grin, before leaning in toward him in a conspiring manner. "I think," I murmured as he, in turn, leaned in closer to me, "that everyone will be a whole lot safer if I stay that way."

Dean's dimples flashed and a low warm laugh puffed from between his lips. "I think that you're probably right," he whispered back in that same conspiring tone.

The bell rang and with a last laughing glance, Dean turned forward in his chair. I could still feel the silly grin on my face but I didn't care. He was just so sweet.

At the end of class, Dean jumped up to head straight to practice, but not before he turned around to me and reminded, "Don't forget, I'm picking you up tomorrow morning so we can help Mrs. Drysdale." I nodded (as if I was likely to forget something like that) and with a quick wave he was gone.

20. One Dark and Rainy Morning

I practically flew to my locker. I needed to remind Peanut that I wouldn't need a ride to school in the morning.

"It's not something I'm likely to forget," she grinned when I caught up with her.

"Now, Peanut," I started to chastise her but she interrupted.

"Don't 'now Peanut' me. I've seen the way you look at him and I've seen the way he looks at you."

I shook my head at her. "We're helping Mrs. Drysdale," I repeated forcefully. "This is not a date."

Peanut gave me a skeptical look and pointed her finger at me. "Well, all I'm saying is that there better not be any kissing in that closet."

"I wish," I mumbled under my breath, but said to Peanut, "Mrs. Drysdale is going to be there, too. How romantic can it possibly get?"

Peanut grimaced. "You've got a point there. Somehow I can't see Mrs. Drysdale inflaming Dean's passions."

"That's gross," I said wincing in disgust, before dissolving into helpless laughter with Peanut, joining in. After a few minutes we were finally able to gather ourselves. With the strictest concentration I gathered the books I needed, stuffed them into my book bag and slammed my locker door shut. "Let's go! I've got to get home to check on Hairy."

"How is that ugly..? I mean darling dog doing?" she asked.

I glared at her to let her know I wasn't fooled by her supposed innocent stutter. The dog had an ugly problem. I knew it. She knew it. My dad definitely knew it. That didn't mean that Hairy needed to know it.

"*He's* doing just fine. I found him an old blanket to sleep on. I had to put him on the screened back porch while I'm at school and Dad is at work. Dad didn't want to take a chance and find out the hard way that he wasn't house trained. So I agreed he should stay there and we'll see how he does."

Peanut grimaced. "Smart move."

I grinned over at her. "Tell me about it. I didn't relish the idea of coming home to poop and pee all over the house." Peanut grimaced all over again.

A few minutes later she dropped me off at the front of my house. With a wave goodbye, I quickly entered through the kitchen door then ran to the porch. Frantic yips assaulted my eardrums.

"It's okay. It's okay," I soothed Hairy as I picked him up into my arms. I glanced around the porch looking for signs of any accidents he may have had. When I didn't find any, I quickly stepped outside and put him down onto the ground. He probably had to go pretty badly. Sure enough, he walked about five steps and did his business. A few steps and a few sniffs later he was doing his other kind of business. "Good boy," I praised him as I scooped him up and carried him back inside.

I played with Hairy and rubbed him and talked to him. I wanted to start on my homework like I usually did, but Hairy had been cooped up all day. I couldn't let him entertain himself just yet. Eventually I tuckered him out. As he slept on the sofa, I started my homework.

Every so often though, my mind would wander off to

thoughts of Dean. Every time I thought of today, I got frustrated all over again. I glanced down at the top I had agonized over wearing all morning. Quite possibly one of the biggest wastes of my time, I decided now. I doubted whether Dean had even noticed it in the few minutes we'd actually spent together.

Of course, I reminded myself, there was always tomorrow. Dean would be picking me up and we would ride to school together. I wondered briefly if David would ride, too. David always drove the two of them to school in a white Mustang. I frowned. I hoped not. Not that I didn't like David or anything like that, I just really wanted some alone time with Dean. If I got that then maybe I could get a better idea about how he felt, because I was pretty convinced that I knew how I felt. I was smitten. He made my heart race and my tummy flutter. He made the smile on my face appear. And he made the smile stick around long after we'd parted. Now all I needed to know was how did I make *him* feel? And better yet, how did he feel about me?

The rest of the evening passed swiftly. I only wished that sleep came as quickly. I lay for what felt like hours in my bed, thinking about tomorrow. I played and replayed one hundred and one different scenarios of how tomorrow could go. They ranged from worst case to best case scenarios. I hoped the best won out. Sighing deeply, I rolled over into a ball and eventually and quite suddenly fell asleep.

Morning dawned dark and rainy. I frowned out the window. Tonight's game would get canceled if it didn't let up by early afternoon. It was absolutely pouring out there. The wind was exceptionally strong as well, I noted as the trees in the backyard swayed in an eerie dance. I hoped Hairy wouldn't be too scared outside on the back porch while I was at school.

I showered and dressed quickly. Rather than dressing for fashion, I decided to dress for practicality sake, due to the downpour of rain and the dirty closet Mrs. Drysdale wanted me to poke around in. As much as I would have liked to be a bit more daring, today of all days, I knew it would probably look ridiculous, especially considering we were expected to do physical labor. So I opted on wearing faded blue jeans and an old but favorite v-neck black t-shirt I'd gotten at a U2 concert.

I pulled my straight dark hair back into a functional ponytail and added my habitual mineral powder, lip gloss and mascara. I stared at my reflection extra critically. I tried to view myself the way Dean would. What did he see when he looked at me? Did he think I was pretty? Did he like brown hair? Did Dean think I was too short or that I wore too much makeup? The longer I looked, the more questions crossed through my mind and the more questions I thought to ask, the more worried I became about the *answers* to all those questions. I turned away from the mirror in desperation. I could *so* be my own worst enemy, I thought with a sigh.

I left my bedroom and stopped by my dad's bedroom door, giving it a light tap. Turning the knob and opening the door, I poked my head inside. "Dad?" I whispered.

"Yeah honey?" he mumbled sleepily into his pillow.

"I'm leaving in a few minutes. I'm helping Mrs. Drysdale today. I wanted to tell you to be careful. It's really nasty out today."

"Always, baby. You be careful, too."

I smiled at him as he buried his head deeper into the pillow. I didn't know how he did it, but he could drop off to sleep in a second and be instantly awake in the next. I closed the door back behind me and went to feed Hairy.

Hairy began greedily chomping his food down as soon as I gave it to him. He acted as if he hadn't eaten in days–which I had to remind myself, he probably *hadn't*. "Poor baby," I said rubbing his hairless backside while he ate. When it appeared that he'd had enough, I grabbed him up and popped him outside the back door and into the heavy rain. I had no intention of following behind him. It was going to be bad enough later when I had to run out to Dean's car.

As if on cue, a horn sounded. Thankfully, Hairy was finished doing his business and was eagerly waiting to be let back inside. I fluffed his blanket and made sure he had plenty of water before giving him a last pat and closing him inside the porch. Running through the house, I grabbed my book bag and ran to the kitchen door. Opening the door, I waved at Dean through the rain to let him know I was coming. With one last deep breath, I jumped down the one step outside the door and ran toward his black Tahoe.

"Thanks," I gasped as I climbed inside. I was only slightly dripping. I swiped at a drop running down my cheek. Thankfully Dean had thoughtfully leaned over and pushed the door open for me, so that when I reached it, it was already open. Those precious few seconds saved me from standing under hundreds of raindrops.

"It's so nasty out!" I gasped, brushing at my arms to wipe away the wetness.

"I know," Dean agreed looking up outside the windshield. "If this keeps up we'll have to postpone the game."

The tone in his voice had me turning and looking at him. I could tell he was upset at the prospect. "Hopefully it will let up," I said with encouragement.

"Hopefully," Dean murmured, flashing me a quick grin and a wink, before returning his attention to backing out of my driveway. In moments we were traveling down the fairly empty streets of Greenville toward school.

"Nice truck," I commented while I tried very hard not to fixate on the wink he had just thrown my way. "Is it yours?" I asked with absentminded curiosity. As I heard my spoken words repeat themselves inside my head, I blushed in embarrassment at my audacity. "I mean," I tried to explain. "David has always driven you two to school in a white Mustang. I was just wondering if that meant this one was yours, and that one was his." I rushed out, before coming to an abrupt stop. "You don't have to answer," I finished with a shake of my head.

"It's okay," Dean quickly assured me. "It's a normal question to ask. And the answer is yes, by the way. This is mine. My parents don't think it's necessary for us to take two cars to school, not to mention a waste of gas, so we double. David prefers driving and I don't really mind either way, so we take his car." Dean flashed me another one of his spectacular grins. "And... *I* save a lot on gas money."

"I thought you were kind of smart," I teased.

"I get by," Dean answered with modesty

"I bet," I quipped back, causing him to chuckle.

Silence descended but it wasn't uncomfortable. I couldn't believe how at ease I felt with him. Everything felt natural. *I* felt natural with him. *I*, who usually guarded every word I spoke, was experiencing an amazingly easy companionship that I'd never been lucky enough to experience before, especially with a guy.

Dean turned into the school entrance. It was raining so hard by this time that I could hardly make out the name, Wolverines, spray painted across the school rock. Instead of driving to the student parking lot, he drove up to the front entrance that had a canopy. "You go ahead and get out here. There's no reason we both should get soaked. I'll meet you outside the library door in a minute."

"Okay," I agreed gathering up my book bag. I turned to look at him. "At least you'll get a great parking spot," I remarked in a 'the glass is half-full' tone of voice, causing him to chuckle.

"At least you didn't say, 'look at the bright side.' I always hate it when someone says that," he teased with a wink. I grinned back at him enjoying the innateness of the conversation. Dean's grin shifted and altered, until he was simply staring at me in what appeared to be deep concentration.

"What?" I questioned. I wiped at my nose. "Do I have something on my face or something?"

A dimple reappeared. "I think I might have already told you this before, but just in case I haven't, I will now. You're sweet," he murmured. "I think you're one of the sweetest girls that I've ever met."

I blushed. "I think you're sweet, too."

Dean chuckled. "That's the kiss of death for a guy, but I won't take offense. I know you meant it in the best possible way."

I blushed again. "Of course I did," I muttered. Then I got my backbone back. "And I happen to think it's a very nice compliment," I assured him. "For a girl *or* a boy. So *you* say thank you and *I'll* say thank you, and we'll both acknowledge to each other just how *freaking* sweet we are."

Dean stared at me for a long moment before bursting into laughter. After a second I joined in.

"Still think I'm *sweet*?" I asked a second later, peeking up at him from beneath my lashes.

Dean winked. "Abso-*freaking*-lutely!"

I clapped my hand over my face in embarrassment and groaned. "Oh my God! I can't believe I actually said that to you!"

"I thought it was cute," Dean teased. "It gave me a little insight."

I frowned in confusion. "What kind of insight?" I wondered aloud to him as I listened to the torrential rain beat down against the roof of the Tahoe.

Dean smiled and completely ignored my question. "Go ahead and hop out. Mrs. Drysdale is going to think we aren't going to show up if you don't get in there."

I gave Dean what I hoped was an intimidating glare. "This ain't over buddy," I warned as I opened the door and climbed out, but before the door completely shut I thought I heard him say, "I'm counting on it."

I watched him drive off before the gusting wind and resultant spray of rain encouraged me to walk inside. I caught a glimpse of my reflection in the school window. My eyes miraculously ignored the wet, windswept mess that was now my hair and instead focused on the animated expression on my face. I marveled at the sight of my wide over bright eyes and the ridiculous smile that seemed super-glued in place. What kind of spell had that boy put me under, I asked myself as I fairly floated into the library?

About five minutes later, Mrs. Drysdale was unlocking the closet door at the back of the musty school library. She turned toward Dean and me. "I'll show you what I want moved out and then I'll show you how I want you to reorganize the things that are left behind."

Dean and I turned to look at each other. The task was starting to sound a lot more complicated, not to mention more back breaking then either of us was first led to believe. I suppressed a groan as Mrs. Drysdale swung the door open. The closet wasn't so much a closet either. It was a tiny room the approximate measurement of Dean's Tahoe. And it was crammed full of stuff.

Dean and I exchanged "what the heck" looks as we stepped inside but we didn't say a word. My immediate thought was that we weren't going to be able to finish this today. Taking a second glance around, I decided we probably wouldn't be finished in a week!

The closet was jam packed with paper Mache art projects, smelly boxes, and other numerous objects that would be found in an older school. Despite the size of the closet, there was very little actual space to maneuver. We stood huddled just inside the room with Mrs. Drysdale while she pointed to various things she wanted moved or thrown out or saved. I was so conscious of Dean's slightly damp but warm length lightly pressed up against mine that I worried I wouldn't remember one instruction that Mrs. Drysdale was giving.

Once Mrs. Drysdale finished explaining, she patted us on our shoulders and calmly walked out, while humming softly to herself.

Dean and I stood where she left us, side by side. Neither

of us spoke for long seconds as we stared around the dimly lit closet and absorbed the weighty task that was set before us.

"So," I finally drawled out on a sigh as I looked up at him. "What do you think?"

Dean looked down at me with pursed lips and whistled. Then in the most solemn tone I'd ever heard him use, he answered. "I think it's time for Mrs. Drysdale to retire."

21. The Kiss

I gasped—then giggled. "I think that's the meanest thing I've ever heard you say!"

Dean cut his eyes at me. "Considering the way I'm feeling right now, it could have been a lot worse. Is she crazy or something?" he asked in a very serious tone. "There's so much stuff here, we'd never get it done in a day, let alone two."

"She can be a bit eccentric," I offered by way of explanation. "Mrs. Drysdale has been here so long that the principal and staff ignore her idiosyncrasies and work around her."

Dean looked at me. "So is that what we're going to do—work around her?"

I nodded. "Basically."

Dean nodded back. "Good. I can live with that. So explain to me how this working around her works," he suggested, as he rolled up imaginary sleeves, showing me he was ready to start.

"I think we should remove the specific things she requested out of the..." I hesitated before gritting out; "*closet*." I took a calming breath then continued, "Then we'll rearrange everything so that it fits in here a little more orderly and gives us," I nudged his shoulder with mine, "a little more room."

Dean laughed down at me, giving me a little nudge back.

"Yeah," he agreed. "I about died too when she unlocked the door and swung it open. This isn't exactly my idea of a closet."

I gave Dean a give me a break look. "Um... I've been to your house and I saw how big your guest bedroom closet is. Now's it's not as big as this I admit, but I did say *guest* bedroom. I have an idea that this closet could fit into your mother's closet with room to spare."

Dean grinned sheepishly. "I'm going to plead the fifth but if it helps, my closet is half the size of this one."

I contemplated that for a moment. "Marginally," I answered as I nodded my head and smiled at him. "I would never have been able to look at you the same way again if I'd found out that your walk-in closet was bigger than mine. There are two things that a man should never have bigger than a woman and one of those things is a closet!"

Dean looked at me strangely. "I'm kind of afraid to ask, but what's the other?"

"Why, a purse, Dean. A purse," I teased with an impish smile, before I started laughing at the expression on his face. "What in the world did you think I was going to say?"

Dean ran his palm down his face and released a gush of air from his lungs. "Believe me when I say that you don't really want to know."

I started laughing harder.

"Okay," I finally said once I had gotten myself under control. I glanced at my watch. "We'd better get started. I think Mrs. Drysdale will notice if we don't at least move something."

Dean and I looked around.

"How about I start pulling down the things she wants out of here and you carry what you can out into the library? Once we've done that, we can start rearranging in here," Dean suggested.

"Sounds good," I said with a shrug.

The next ten minutes we worked in companionable silence. We started dragging and carrying the old dusty boxes and desks that Mrs. Drysdale had specifically requested be moved, trashing the years old art projects, and rearranging an assortment of boxes and equipment that she wanted to keep.

"You don't think she'll expect us to carry all that mess out to the trash, do you?" Dean asked me at one point.

"Nah," I answered shaking my head and blowing a strand of hair of out my face. "I'm sure she'll get the janitor to move it out."

"Why doesn't she get the janitor to do *all* of it?" he asked me with curiosity as he hefted one of the larger boxes and carried it out of the closet. "Why does she always ask you to do this stuff?"

I shrugged. "I often wondered the same thing until one time she told me Mr. Potter—he's the janitor by the way—was so over worked that she didn't like to bother him with her little errands."

"You know that doesn't really make any sense," Dean said as he carried another old box out of the closet. "And this isn't exactly a *little* project."

"I have to agree with you about that," I laughed, stuffing a broken clay pot into the trash can Mrs. Drysdale had so thoughtfully set up for us outside the closet door. "The things she normally asks me to help her with," I continued, "aren't nearly this daunting. I'm beginning to wonder if the job became bigger the moment she volunteered you to help."

"Well if it did, then I'm sorry," he offered in apology.

"That's okay. I forgive you," I said and patted him on his back. It felt warm and hard and slightly damp from the rain. I lifted my hand away and rubbed it against my thigh but the impression lingered. How strange, I thought.

Silence returned as we finished carrying out the few remaining objects Mrs. Drysdale had instructed us to remove. I walked back into the closet to start rearranging, while Dean organized all the paraphernalia we'd stacked in the library so that no one would trip over it. A few minutes later Dean joined me. We continued to work quickly and efficiently so that we could make it to first period on time.

We were both pulling at an old filing cabinet that was sitting cockeyed in the corner, when the sound of the door slamming shut ricocheted around the room. The noise was so startling I jumped and screamed. Hollow laughter could be heard from behind the door before it faded away. I looked over toward Dean but he was already lunging at the door and trying to open it. It wouldn't budge.

"It's locked or jammed or something," Dean said twisting and pulling on the knob with all his strength.

"You're kidding?" I gasped, with my hand to my heart. It was still pounding in fright.

"I wish," he said, as he finally gave up trying to open the door. He ran his fingers through his dark spiky hair, making the ends stand up in every direction.

I looked at the door, then back at Dean. "Why did it do that? Why did it slam shut?"

"I think," Dean said. "That someone slammed it shut on purpose. Did you hear laughter right after it happened?"

I stared at him while I recalled the last few seconds. "Are you saying that you actually think someone did this on purpose as some kind of joke?" I finally gasped out.

Dean shrugged. "I'm not sure about the joke part, but yeah, I think this was done intentionally."

I paced in the tiny confines of the room. "Thank God the light switch is on the inside of the room." I shuddered, imagining how terrifying this ordeal would be if we had been trapped in the dark. It was already a little spooky as it was.

"Someone is going to notice all of that stuff out in the library and wonder about it. They'd have to figure out that it came from inside the closet and come investigate further." I remarked to Dean, looking up at him for confirmation.

Dean winced slightly. "Not necessarily. I just finished moving all of it further back so that no one would accidentally trip over it. Whoever sees the stuff will probably assume it's been there for a while."

"Well, that's great," I snapped. I looked over at Dean and immediately lay my hand on his arm in a placating gesture. "I wasn't snapping at you. I don't blame you. I blame whoever decided to pull such an asinine prank. Now him, I blame."

"It's okay," Dean assured me.

After a moment, I crossed my arms protectively across my chest and started pacing again. Very little time passed before I stopped and once again looked at Dean. *He* had continued to stand by the doorway, staring at his feet with his hands in his pockets. My stillness and continued silence made him glance up at me.

"Who do you think did this?" I asked him with curiosity. That particular question had me stumped.

Dean twisted his lips into the closest thing to a smirk I'd ever seen from him. "I could hazard a guess," he growled.

I stepped closer toward him and reached my hand out to lay it on his bicep. "Who?" I asked. I'd never seen Dean look so angry. I wanted to comfort him but I didn't know how, which was pretty funny, because I really could have gone for some comforting myself. "Who would have done this and why?" I repeated.

Dean took his hands out of his pockets causing me to automatically remove my hand from his arm, but before I could take a step back, Dean was reaching out and grabbing my hand between his palms. "I can only think of one person that would get some kind of sick kick out of doing this not only to me but to you," Dean offered quietly, staring down into my eyes and watching my face as realization dawned.

"Chad?" I breathed out. "Chad!" I said more emphatically.

"That would be my guess," Dean agreed with a nod as he continued to maintain possession of my hand. "I don't know for sure," Dean tried to placate me. "It's not like I saw him but...."

I snatched my hand out of Dean's and started pacing. "But it's the sort of thing he'd do," I finished for him.

"Hey," Dean sighed, catching hold of my hand again as I made another sweep by him, stopping me in my tracks. "After Friday night, I'd agree Chad could be capable of a lot," he agreed. "But you have to admit that this is a pretty short sighted plan on his part. I mean, yeah we're trapped... but that's it. No more, no less. Eventually Mrs. Drysdale is going to come and check on us and then we're out of here."

In the next instant Dean released my hand but, before I could miss the comfort of his touch, he wrapped me up into his strong arms. It felt so good. It felt wonderful! He'd held me on Friday night but I had been in shock then, soaking wet and downright miserable. But now, though I was kind of scared, I wasn't scared enough to not reap the full benefits of Dean Scott's healing arms and appreciate the feel of his hard, lean body against mine.

"Chad's a jerk," I mumbled into Dean's neck. A part of me felt like a hypocrite because right at this moment, I quite possibly could have thanked Chad if he had been standing in front of me. Of course, the other part of me knew that Chad had not done this out of the kindness of his heart, which did make him a big, big jerk.

"He is," Dean agreed from over top of my head. "He's probably thinking that if he can keep me stuck in here through at least first period and make me miss class without an approved excuse, then I'd be benched and the coach would have no other option than to let him play tonight."

"Why would you be benched?" I asked, leaning my head back and looking up into his crystal eyes.

Dean smiled down at me for a second before explaining, "School rules prohibit a player from missing any class on game day. If a player misses without a prior approved excuse, then he's benched for the entire game without exception."

I rolled my eyes. "I get it! It's pretty stupid, but I get it."

Dean's smile grew. "Yep! Like I said, Chad didn't put much thought into this plan. I think it was more a plan of opportunity rather than strategy. He probably saw us standing in here together and reacted without thought."

"I think Chad does most things without thought," I commented while wrinkling my nose.

"You know," Dean said looking down at me, his arms tightening perceptibly. "You look kind of cute when you do that."

My heartbeat accelerated at a rapid speed. "Do what?" I whispered.

"Wrinkle your nose like that," Dean murmured.

I wrinkled it again in confusion, causing Dean to chuckle, which promptly made me blush. "I didn't do that on purpose!" I denied in a rush.

Dean chuckled again. "I know. You do it when you're confused or if you're making a joke but you're not sure the other person will think it's funny. And sometimes like now," he added. "You do it when you're disgusted with someone... like Chad."

I stared at Dean in wonder. "You've noticed all of that?" I whispered.

Dean's dimples flashed. "Oh yeah," he whispered back. "I've noticed lots of things."

His words made me feel brave and a tad bit daring. I sucked in my breath. "I've noticed something about you, too." I dared to say to him.

"You have?" Dean murmured while looking down at me. His eyes wandered from my eyes, down to my lips and back again.

I felt a light blush rise along my cheeks but I fought off my shyness. "Yeah," I murmured. "I have." I felt my own eyes lowering to Dean's mouth and watched while his lips moved while he spoke.

"And what would that be?" he finally asked in a soft, husky tone that spoke to me more than his actual words.

For a second, I became so lost in his eyes and his voice that I lost my train of thought. I really couldn't believe that any of this was happening to me. That unexciting and unadventurous little old me was flirting, actually and quite intentionally, flirting with Dean Scott while standing in his arms inside of a locked closet. The sheer lack of reality to the entire situation emboldened me and I found myself murmuring, "I've noticed you never call me by my name."

Dean smiled a sweet, sweet smile. The skin around his eyes crinkled and his crystal eyes twinkled down at me. Both his expression and voice were tender when he finally responded.

"I don't know your name," he said simply.

I pulled back a little to look up at him with a frown. "Of course you do," I said in a tone that betrayed my confusion.

"No," he said with a slight shake of his head. "I know your *nickname*," he clarified with a slight nod to his head. "But I don't know your *name*."

I drew in a deep breath. I was flabbergasted, and I didn't know what to say in response. Then the obvious thing to say came to mind.

"My name's Jenna," I whispered.

"Hello, Jenna," Dean whispered back.

And as if in slow motion I watched Dean's face lower slowly towards mine. My legs, of their own volition, stood up on tiptoes, meeting him halfway. In the next heartbeat, our lips touched in the softest of butterfly greetings before retreating. I opened my eyes to find Dean's eyes searching mine. He must have found what he was searching for because in the next instant he was drawing me closer to him and lowering his head for a second kiss, and if at all possible, a better kiss.

The warmth and softness of his lips came as a surprise. Though I'd never kissed a boy before, I had often imagined what it would be like. Nothing in my imagination could compare with this though. It was..."

A slight click and a whoosh of air interrupted my wanderings as well as the kiss. Dean and I immediately and guiltily sprang apart and looked towards the door. My stomach lurched when I saw Mr. Blakely, our principal, standing there with Mrs. Drysdale, as well as a handful of students.

"Oh my God!" I whispered under my breath. I couldn't say anything other than that. I stared wide-eyed from Mr. Blakely to Mrs. Drysdale to the students gaping open mouthed at us. I couldn't wrap my mind around the entire situation. Not only had I just had my first kiss, but I had been caught, in a closet at school no less, by the principal and what felt like half of the student body.

I looked over at Dean, with the hope that somehow, looking at him would make everything miraculously okay. But Dean didn't look back at me and no answer to my predicament presented itself. I really hadn't thought that being a teenage girl in America could get any tougher. Then I looked at the expression on the principal's face and I knew that it could.

Coming Soon!
Behind Closet Doors
Book 2 in The Chunky Girl Chronicles

LaVergne, TN USA
14 December 2010
208686LV00003B/36/P